TROUBLE RIDES THE WIND

**Center Point
Large Print**

**This Large Print Book carries the
Seal of Approval of N.A.V.H.**

TROUBLE RIDES THE WIND

B. M. Bower

Center Point Publishing
Thorndike, Maine

This Center Point Large Print edition
is published in the year 2005 by arrangement with
Golden West Literary Agency.

The text of this Large Print edition is unabridged. In other
aspects, this book may vary from the original edition. Printed in
Thailand. Set in 16-point Times New Roman type.

ISBN 1-58547-512-2

Library of Congress Cataloging-in-Publication Data

Bower, B. M., 1874-1940.
   Trouble rides the wind / B. M. Bower.--Center Point large print ed.
      p. cm.
   ISBN 1-58547-512-2 (lib. bdg. : alk. paper)
   1. Large type books. I. Title.

PS3503.O8193T76 2005
812'.54--dc22

2004011963

CONTENTS

CHAPTER ONE
MYSTERY BLOWS CHIP'S WAY

On a certain forenoon in the month of May, young Chip Bennett loped into Dry Lake with his nose about the color of a freshly ripened prune. His bloodshot eyes watered in the north wind and his ears were red and swollen with cold, all because the wind that had been balmy with false promises of spring when he left the Flying U that morning had switched treacherously to the coldest corner of the globe—and Chip had foolishly left his heavy sourdough coat at home.

Pulling up in front to the blacksmith shop, he tossed the two parts of a broken bridle bit to the smithy who had been brought to the doorway by the sound of Chip's headlong arrival.

"Say, John, how long will it take you to mend that bit?"

The blacksmith spat away from the wind. "Wel-l," he said, inspecting the break, "you come back in about an hour and I'll try and have it for yuh. Got some work on a wagon wheel—"

Chip eased the reins and his horse jumped into a gallop. "I'll be back in an hour, John," he flung over his shoulder, and was off up the rutted roadway that served as a street for the main part of town.

One glance he sent toward the hitch rail in front of Rusty Brown's saloon, shivered at the bleakness of its wind-swept exposure, and reined across to the new livery stable, which was closer and on the same side of the street as the saloon.

"Hey, Squint!" he shouted cheerfully, "take this cayuse of mine and stand him in a stall, will yuh? Never mind unsaddling—I'll want him again in an hour or so."

"I sure will," drawled the hostler, buttoning his mackinaw as he stepped outside. He said it to Chip's back, for already that chilly young cowpuncher was off his horse and taking long steps across a vacant lot to the saloon which he had decided would be the warmest place in town just then.

Within the doorway his interest centered at once upon the heat waves wrinkling upward from the pot-bellied stove that stood between a round card table and a booth which was the saloon's one claim to elegance. Here, in the gracious warmth, he unbuttoned his coat, stuffed his leather gloves carelessly into a pocket and leaned back luxuriously in an armchair, his spurred boots thrust out to the nickeled rail around the stove's dingy base.

The change from biting wind to the stuffy heat of that corner relaxed his muscles as a powerful narcotic would do, weighting his eyelids to a drowsy content. He slid farther down upon his shoulder blades, leaned his head against the partition and prepared himself for the luxury of a nap. The hum of lowered voices within the booth at his back carried no meaning, served even to increase his sense of drowsy comfort.

No idea of listening entered his languorous thoughts, yet the mumble of one voice presently disturbed him, like the persistent hum of a mosquito circling just over his face. With no attempt to identify the sound, it nevertheless held him back, kept him from slipping into the delicious half-slumber he had set himself to enjoy.

Then gradually he knew it for the voice of Dunk Whittaker, the Flying U's new partner. A rasping, supercilious voice that never failed to cause a prickling sensation at the nape of Chip's neck, as if his hair wanted to stand up in a fighting ruff. It had that effect now, even while he was half-asleep and only dimly aware of the irritation.

But presently he roused himself to wonder what Dunk was doing in Rusty Brown's place, when he was supposed to be in Helena, running his bank. He wasn't due in Dry Lake for another month, at least. Why, Chip remembered, it wasn't a week since Dunk had made his periodical visit to Flying U ranch and had left again, too full of business to stay longer than one day and night. It certainly was queer—

Then a nasal voice with a whine of alarm broke in upon the mumble. "That ain't the way you put it before. By—I never bargained on nothin' like that! Looks to me like I'm bein' framed into the pen myself, instead of—"

"Shut up! Nobody's framing you. This will only be a matter of form; what you fellows would call a grandstand play," Dunk Whittaker's voice interrupted him. "We'll have you out in no time, at all."

"Well, I don't like the idee a damn bit. Why can't you tip me off when you go to make your killin', an' let me pull out? You'll have your evidence all planted—"

Dunk's low contemptuous laugh answered that, and there was something about state's witness, spoken too low for Chip to catch. The other started to say something, was stopped with another low argumentative sentence, and the final command clearly given. "Get back down there and finish—" the remainder was blurred under a scuffing of boots, as the two apparently got up to leave. It was plain the conference was over.

With his hat tilted down over his thin rather high nose, Chip waited. He heard Dunk go to the bar and buy cigars, then he walked past the stove and on out of the saloon, with the arrogant swing of his shoulders which the Happy Family had come to hate so impotently, without exactly knowing why. And because he would not condescend to look about him as he went, Dunk did not see Chip sitting there behind the stove, watching him from under the brim of his hat.

Just then the side door slammed. Evidently Dunk's companion had chosen the more inconspicuous exit at the end of the bar and just beyond the booth. Chip glanced toward the window, saw that the crudely painted glass gave no view of the outdoors save through the upper sash, and on a sudden impulse he rose and made his way hurriedly to the door.

He was too late to learn anything definite. Dunk Whittaker's expensive overcoat was just disappearing into the general store a few rods up the street. At the hitch rail a man in a long sourdough coat and a fur cap was mounting a chunky brown horse. Chip squinted at the brand, glanced sharply at the man. But the fellow's back was turned and he did not look around as he rode off down the street. Chip watched until rider and the dust he raised whipped around the corner of the blacksmith shop, then with a snort of disgust, he turned back into the saloon, telling himself it was none of his business, anyway.

But for all that, the thing stuck in his mind. His pool that day would have tickled the Happy Family, for he played three games in succession and got stuck for the drinks each time; an unheard-of performance for young Chip Bennett, who was known to have an uncannily accurate eye and a hand that never lost its rocklike steadiness with a billiard cue—or a gun.

Thoroughly disgruntled, he got his mended bridle bit and rode home, too preoccupied with the mystery to curse the bitter wind that harried him all the way.

CHAPTER TWO
A STRAW IN THE WIND

"Say, I'd give a dollar to know who Dunk was talking to and who he was framing yesterday," Chip stated abruptly next day, when he and Weary Davidson happened to be alone in the blacksmith shop at the Flying U.

Weary glanced up inquiringly from the spur shank he was straightening, and his eyes rested upon Chip's moody face bent over the bridle bit that had been mended too hurriedly and needed quite a lot of smoothing and polishing before he would ask any horse in his string to carry it in his mouth.

"Dunk, you say? What's eatin' on yuh, Chip? No fortune-tellers on this range, far as I know. Dunk probably talked to a hundred men yesterday in his office, maybe more. And if he framed anybody, he likely framed every darned one—not that I'm any knocker. What's put that idea in your head, anyway?"

The fine, sensitive curve in Chip's mouth straightened. He gave a snort that carried a complexity of meanings. "I don't need any fortune-teller to know he was framing somebody, but I certainly would like to know the name of the framee, all right. Sounded like Dunk was building himself a murder, if you ask me."

Weary forgot to pump the bellows and the coals went black on the forge. He stared at Chip, then suddenly laughed. "Mamma! I darned near swallowed the hook that time. You sure sounded like you meant that. Pull it on Slim and Happy Jack, why don't yuh?"

Chip gave him a look of reproach. "Oh, it's no josh. I did mean it. I was in at Rusty's, thawing out, and I certainly heard Dunk making bad medicine for somebody. Damnedest frame-up you ever heard."

"No! You honestly mean it, Chip?" Weary let go of the bellows handle and got out his tobacco and cigarette papers. "If you're just stringin' me, I'll beat your fool brains out with your own boots. If you ain't, I'll say Rusty Brown's is a darned public place to frame any crooked work in. Dunk must be crazy." He sifted tobacco into the little paper trough in his fingers. "If it was him," he added doubtfully, looking up under his hatbrim.

"It was Dunk, all right. I'd know that voice in hell on

a hot night. The way I happened to overhear what was said, I was sitting back behind the stove in that corner, kinda sprawled out, with my head leaned back against that fancy boxstall Rusty's built in that end of the room. Dunk and some jasper he was talking to happened to be inside, holding a private conflab, feeling safe enough because the saloon was empty on that side—except for me, and they evidently hadn't heard me come in. Only for a few fellows over around the pool tables, there wasn't anybody in the place."

"Yeah, I can see how they could have it to themselves, just about. But you bet your life I wouldn't hive up like that to talk private—"

"Well, it was about the only place in town, when you figure it out. Way the wind was howling down off the bench, they couldn't very well stand outside—Rusty's is just about the only meeting place there is in town, remember, where it would look natural. Anyway, that's where they were. I didn't pay any attention to 'em at first, except I knew it was Dunk in there and I hoped to the Lord he wasn't headed for the ranch again."

"Couldn't be. Old Man got a big, long letter from him—like a deed or some darn document. It was in the mail sack you brought out," Weary observed, tossing his match stub into the forge.

"I saw that myself. No, he wasn't headed for the ranch, but I guess there was no law against his riding on the same train that brought the letter. Anyway, he certainly was in that booth, and the way he talked made Judas look like a saint. If I knew who he was framing—"

"Didn't you get any line on the deal atall?"

"No. I didn't come alive to the situation soon enough, or I might have got the whole play. This jasper Dunk was talking to was beefing, first I paid any attention. He didn't want to get pulled into jail for something or other. He said Dunk oughta tip him off when the killing was to take place, so he could skin out. And Dunk said that wouldn't do, because they'd need him for a state's witness."

"Tip him off before the killing, hunh?" grunted Weary. "It sure don't seem like Dunk Whittaker, with all the money he's got, would hardly dare to get mixed up in anything like that." He looked at Chip suddenly and grinned. "Say, you didn't by any chance get your drinks mixed, did yuh?"

From his own book of papers Chip singled out a leaf, tore off a tiny strip from the side and rolled it into a pellet. "Don't get funny," he said shortly. "This thing has got me running around in circles. Damn it, if I knew who they were out to get—"

"Nobody up around Helena, or Dunk wouldn't be off out in this country framing it," mused Weary. "Must be somebody around in this locality. Say, what kinda lookin' guy was the other fellow? Anybody you know?"

"That's the hell of it, Weary. I never got a squint at him. While I was waiting for him to pass me—Dunk did, and never looked my way—that other jasper sneaked out that side door around behind the booth. Time I got to the front door for a look at him, he could have ducked into the store or the restaurant or anywhere, most."

"No line on him atall?"

"Not unless he was the fellow I saw climbing on a horse out at the hitchrail. I didn't get to see his face. Wore a long sourdough coat and a fur cap—kinda late in the season, wearing a fur cap along the first of May, is why I noticed that. He was riding a chunky brown that didn't look as if it had ever seen a currycomb—"

"That kinda sounds like a feller I met that time I rode down and stayed with the Duncan boys a day or two last winter. Name of Pete Riser. Pete wears a fur cap with ear muffs on it, and he rides a chunky brown—"

"Brand looked to me like an O Bar, or a D Bar maybe. The hair was so long and matted I couldn't tell for sure," Chip hopefully supplied.

But Weary shook his head. "I couldn't say what the brand is. But shucks! What would a darned plutocrat like Dunk Whittaker be making medicine with a guy like that for? Pete's just a wolfer that's been down along the river all winter. He was there at the Duncan's, and he'd just run across a pack of eighteen wolves, he claimed. Brought in a hindquarter of beef; a lone yearling he said the wolves had hamstrung and got down, just before he jumped 'em. He bled the yearlin' and skinned out a hindquarter and brought it in, and the liver. We had fried liver for supper."

"Did you find out where the fellow was stopping?"

"Well, no, I didn't. But from the way he talked, I took it he's down in there close somewhere." Weary rubbed off his cigarette ash against the anvil. "I sure can't see him and Dunk teamin' up together," he added reflectively. "Musta been some other guy you heard in there."

"Yes, that could happen, all right," Chip conceded. "It's as I told you,—the man might have gone in the restaurant before I got outside to look. This man in the fur cap struck me as being a logical suspect, though. He certainly didn't come out of Rusty's front door and he was just untying his horse. If he were the man I heard go out that side door, he'd just about have time to get to his horse when I spotted him. Of course, it's only a guess on my part."

He smoked in gloomy silence for a minute, watching Weary make ready to resume his work. "I wish to thunder I could forget the whole thing," he added disgustedly. "But damn it, how do I know it isn't someone right in this outfit Dunk's scheming to have bumped off?"

Weary laughed at that. "Mamma! It could be me, easy enough," he chuckled. "Come right down to it, I guess Dunk would like to see us all pushing up the daisies. But that ain't saying he's making his plans to beef the whole outfit. Nope, Dunk would rob widder women and orphans, and chances are he does, all right; but it don't stand to reason he'd risk his neck at murder. He's too sharp for that." His hammer clanged down on steel with a cheerful clink. "Better cut out worrying about it," he advised amiably. "Anyway, maybe you heard crooked. Folks do, half the time."

"What I heard was crooked enough," Chip retorted, "but I heard it straight and don't you forget it." He ground his cigarette stub under his heel and turned toward the door. "Go ahead and be a damned optimist, if you want to. I'll keep my thoughts to myself, after this."

He did. He kept his thoughts so strictly to himself that Weary let the whole thing slip from his mind, and when Chip saddled his private horse Mike early the next Sunday morning and rode off without a word to anyone, it never occurred to Weary that he might still be worrying about that mysterious conversation he had overheard.

Chip was playing a hunch. During the hours when he lay awake at night, trying to think his way to some reasonable explanation of Dunk's scheming, the idea had struck him that if the man in the fur cap were Pete Riser the wolfer, and if he had been the man in the booth with Dunk Whittaker, half owner of the Flying U, then their conversation might very easily concern the Duncan brothers, Steve and Bob.

The reason for that guess lay in Dunk's ruthless methods of doing business generally and his application of those methods in his effort to add more land to the Flying U holdings. He had begun by taking every possible advantage of the land-leasing law, new at that time and a boon to stockmen. By acquiring leases, he had managed to surround several small ranches with barbed wire, artfully weaving his web of wire so as to leave the rancher no outlet and, wherever possible, no water for his small herds.

Once effectually bottled up, the rancher was glad to sell land and cattle for whatever he could get—and that was not much, when Dunk Whittaker fixed the price.

Bob and Steve Duncan had been shut in by new

17

fences, but they had not sold out to the Flying U. When they no longer had access to the open range, they had quietly moved their little bunch of cattle down into the edge of the Badlands, taking possession of a choice piece of river bottom, well protected with rough country and all unsurveyed. Here they built sheds, corrals and a cabin, and here they lived, lonely but triumphant, returning to their home ranch only during the haying season.

The Happy Family had laughed up their sleeves and openly wished the Duncans luck. They suspected that J. G. laughed with them, though they never caught him at it and could only guess what he thought of his business partner's land grabbing. They knew well enough that he was not a party to it and gave Whittaker the management only because he had made a heavy cash investment and was a banker and therefore better qualified to handle the business than Jim Whitmore, whose entire system of bookkeeping reposed in the tally book he carried in his vest pocket.

They knew the Duncans were willing to sell the home ranch, and that if it had been left to J. G., he would have paid them their price if he could afford it, or left them alone and been a good neighbor. Whittaker offered them less than half what the place was worth, and when they laughed in his face, he wove his web like the spider he was and waited, saying no more about it.

For months now the deal had stood deadlocked and the ranch was showing signs of neglect. It was a shame, too, because it would have made a splendid addition to the Flying U spread. It lay down near the mouth of Flying U creek, with plenty of good hay meadows, plenty of shelter and water—plenty of everything except acreage for range now that all the land around it had been leased by the Flying U. It would have made an ideal line camp. But there it lay, its high gate padlocked, the hinges rusting from disuse.

There might be no connection whatever between the Duncan boys and that sinister conference in Rusty Brown's private booth, but Chip meant to make sure. He headed that morning as straight for the river as the sharp-nosed pinnacles and steep ridges would permit, disdaining the main-traveled road. For two hours he rode steadily, then rounded a bold, rocky point and came out into the river basin which was his destination.

A head was thrust inquiringly from the doorway and a voice shouted in surprised welcome, "Well, look what blowed down the canyon! Come right in, old-timer! You're just in time!"

Chip swung out of the saddle and went in where Steve's brother Bob hailed him boisterously. It was a monotonous life they lived, down in that shut-in valley, and they saw few riders during the long winter months—and not so many during the summer, either; though if they had seen hundreds every day, Chip Bennett would still have been a welcome visitor.

They did not ask what his errand was. That, they would have said, was none of their business. And for reasons of his own, Chip did not tell them. So far as they could see, he had no errand other than the impulse to pay a friendly visit; for he had a horror of being thanked for favors or of being considered an interfering cuss, and his talent for keeping his own counsel was famous among his fellows. They'd never be able to say he'd gone hunting a mare's nest, he told himself. They wouldn't if he could help it—and he thought he could.

CHAPTER THREE
GOSSIP WITH A MEANING

For the third time Steve swung the Duncan coffeepot invitingly toward Chip. Twice it was permitted to tilt over his cup, but this time he shook his head and pushed the box he was sitting on back against the wall, so that he could lean comfortably against the peeled logs and smoke his after-dinner cigarette. With apparent aimlessness, he took up the desultory range gossip where it had been momentarily interrupted.

"Bothered much with wolves down in here last winter? I saw some pretty big tracks as I was coming along in the breaks; some of 'em fresh."

Bob had his jackknife out, opening the small blade. "Wel-l," he drawled, as he shaved a splinter off the table edge for a toothpick, "I shot me a couple, and Steve, he got one. We ain't been bothered as much as you'd think. Wolfer down below here has been keepin' 'em pretty much on the run."

"Yeah, Pete must have fifteen, twenty pelts. Last

time, he claims to of got four," Steve supplemented idly.

"I've heard of him," Chip observed with just the right shade of indifference. "Been stopping here, hasn't he?"

The Duncan brothers exchanged a look which Chip couldn't read. "He stops when it's my turn to wrangle the grub," Steve grinned. "Pete, he don't take much to Bob's cookin'."

"Well, I don't aim to have him take to it," Bob defended himself. "The way he lays into our grub makes me tired—and it ain't because I'm Scotch, either."

"You shouldn't begrudge a man what he eats," Steve drawled with exasperating calm.

"I don't. Or I wouldn't, if he et like a human," Bob turned to their visitor. "It's like this: Steve and I are light eaters." He waved a hand toward the remains of a well-planned, well-cooked meal. "We've got to have lots of fruit and canned veg'tables, or we're both fightin' our stummicks all the time. I can't git along on bacon and beans and boiled meat three times a day—"

"You can't git along on nothin'," Steve flung in pettishly.

"I can too, on the right grub. I ain't had a bilious spell all winter. But Pete Riser—I'll tell yuh what he does. He comes packin' in a hull quarter uh beef he's traded deer meat to some rancher for, and then he sets down and gorges himself on can peas and sauce and light bread. Why—" Bob leaned forward to emphasize his tale of woe "—he'll stay a week and eat nothin' but

21

fancy grub! Time after time, I've seen him git away with a hull bucket of stewed apricots—or prunes or apples, whatever we've got—at one settin'!"

"Is that right!" Chip's tone was sufficiently sympathetic. "I certainly would like to watch him perform, some time. You mean to say he won't eat good beef, after buying it and packing it in?"

"Not if he can git anything else. If he don't like meat, what the hell is he always buyin' it for? He knows damn well we ain't no meat eaters ourselves. A good steak now and then, mebby, but that's about all."

"Where did you say he hangs out when he isn't here?" Chip hoped they would not wonder at the question.

"Oh, he's got a cabin about four miles down river, that he calls headquarters. But he ranges all over." Bob's gesture took in the entire country north of the river. "I ain't seen him for a week, thank God."

"I believe I saw him in town yesterday," Chip observed indifferently. "Does he ride a chunky brown, branded D Bar, or maybe O Bar?"

"D Bar. In town, hunh? Hope the son of a gun eats dried apples till he swells up and busts!" Bob caught Chip's questioning grin and explained. "Last time Pete was here, I was just startin' to clean me a mess of dried apples. And damned if he didn't set there and swaller 'em fast as I could cut out the specks and cores!"

"Just the same, he packed in a nice hunk of loin when he come," Steve pointed out. "Traded for it up on Dog Creek."

Bob snorted. "I wish to thunder he'd trade for a wagon-load of dried fruit and stay home till it's all et."

Chip carefully scraped the ash off his cigarette. "Seems funny to me he'd be packing beef in to you fellows. Doesn't he know you've got plenty of cattle and could kill what you want?"

This time it was Steve, the younger brother, who gave the snort. "Hell, we've got cattle, but we ain't got any meat," he declared, bantering Bob good-naturedly. "Only when the wolves pulled down a couple of yearlin's last winter and Pete happened along in time to scatter 'em, we ain't the first idea of what Duncan beef tastes like! Bob, he'd set and starve before he'd go out and beef a critter with his brand on it."

He was joking, just as he always joked about Bob's stingy ways, which existed only in his catalogue of jibes. But Chip looked at him, half tempted to tell him such talk was risky, even in a joke. Let the wrong pair of ears listen, and the Duncan boys might be called a name they did not merit.

Bob took up the challenge. "Hell, we couldn't eat a hull beef all winter and you know it!" he declared. "That darned fruit hawg ain't give us a chance to get meat hungry, anyway." He got up and started to clear the table. "Steve devils me a lot, but he knows damn well I'd kill a beef if we wanted meat."

Chip followed that up. "What does this Pete Riser keep on packing in beef for, when he knows you don't need it?" he asked curiously.

"Oh, damned if I know," Bob replied, slightly bored with the subject. "Yes, I do too. He wants an excuse to belly up to our table and gorge himself on our kinda grub. Kinda figures a hunk of beef'll square up for what he eats, I guess." He took the dishpan down off the wall behind the stove, dipped in water from a bucket near by and set it to heat.

Chip clung to the subject. "Why doesn't he pack in a deer now and then?"

Steve answered that. "Oh, Pete can't stomach venison, since he got stormbound one winter and had to live on straight deer meat for about six weeks. Can't stand the smell of it cookin', even. When he kills a deer, he packs it over to some of them ranchers on Dog Creek and trades it for beef."

"Oh, I see." Chip believed then that he did. He pinched out his cigarette stub, got up and tossed it outside and reached for the flour-sack dish-towel hanging on a spike behind the stove. While Bob washed plates and cups, Chip wiped them and set them back in the cupboard.

He had finished all but the knives and forks when he injected a new note into the desultory conversation. "Oh, say! Ever hear any more outa J. G.'s partner about buying your ranch?"

Bob gave his characteristic snort. "No, and we ain't likely to. Last time he come after me about it, I shore sent him off with a bug in his ear."

Steve laughed reminiscently. "Yeah, Bob sure unloaded all he had on his mind that time. Told Whittaker where to head in at, and don't you forget it. He stood there and took it, too. Bob called him every kinda skunk and range hawg he could think of—and

24

Bob, he sure has got a prolific mind when it comes to cussin' a man out thorough."

Chip laughed. "And what did Dunk say to that?"

"Not a damned word. Just kinda lifted the corner of his lip at Bob in that kioty sneer of his and turned and walked off. And that," grinned Steve, "is the last we've saw or heard of high-collar Whittaker. I been kinda dis-appointed, too. I've been wantin' to tell him a few things, myself."

"He shore found out he had the wrong bull by the tail when he tackled me and Steve," Bob bragged. "He might bluff some of the other nesters, but there's one ranch he'll never get for a song." He wiped out the dishpan and hung it back on its nail. "I ain't got nothin' against J. G.," he added apologetically. "He's shore as white as they come. But since he's been lettin' Dunk Whittaker run the business—"

"He doesn't, any more than he has to. Dunk's got the money, you want to remember. He's a banker too, and that makes it worse. J. G. feels as if Dunk has got a right to handle the money end and let him run the outfit. All that rustling, a year or so ago, and then that hard winter, kinda put a crimp in the Flying U. He had to take in a partner with capital, so he could get on his feet and build up the cattle faster. Now, I guess he wishes he'd taken his loss and worried through best way he could. Don't ever think he's the one hogging the range."

"We don't," Bob promptly assured him. "We know who's doin' all the dirty work. That Whittaker is a polecat. I wouldn't put nothin' past him. Sure as God

25

made little apples, he'll git the Flyin' U in bad before he's through."

"No, he won't—he'll never have the chance." Chip scooped his hat off the bunk and set it on his head. "Well, I'll have to be drifting, I guess." He got into his sourdough coat, pulled his gloves out of a pocket and put them on. "We'll be seeing you fellows on roundup, I suppose."

Now that he had learned all they could tell him, he was in a hurry to be gone. They followed him to the corral, urging him not to be in such a damned rush, but to stay and have supper after awhile. It was Sunday, wasn't it? His time was his own.

"Sure, it's Sunday, but I've got things to do." Chip's tone was brusque. He gathered up the reins, swung into the saddle.

"Well, don't go off mad," Steve drawled a parting jibe.

Chip grinned down at the two. "Not mad, just in a hell of a hurry. Well, be good to yourselves, boys."

Fingers thrust into their overall pockets and thumbs hooked over the edges, they stood mystified by his sudden departure. "Wonder what he wanted?" Steve voiced the question in both minds as they turned back to the cabin, blowing the white steam of their breath before them.

"Lord only knows," Bob said wistfully. "Funny kid. Had something on his mind, all right. He shore never rode away off down here just to pass the time of day." He spat off to one side, hitting a blackened patch of old snow lying in the shade of a rock. "Talk till you're black in the face, and you'd never find out by askin', though. There's one feller that shore can keep his mouth shut in seven different languages."

"Damn good habit to have," Steve opined, and pushed open the cabin door. "Wisht he'd stayed, though. He's quiet, but he sure is good company. Gives a feller a chance to get a lot of talk out of his system."

CHAPTER FOUR
THE WOLFER SHOWS FIGHT

About four miles to Pete Riser's cabin, Bob had said. Chip hurried, for he had spent more time than he had intended at the Duncan place. He didn't consider it time wasted, however, for he believed now he understood in a general way what it was Dunk had been talking about, and who he had been planning to get. It wouldn't be the first time a small rancher had been framed as a rustler and his land and cattle taken from him, either as a means of settling the case out of court, or on a forced sale to cover the cost of hiring lawyers. That much he thought he understood well enough.

Where the "killing" came in, he did not know, though he hoped to find out if he could catch Pete Riser at home. It was pretty safe to guess that Pete would have a hard time proving just where and to whom he had traded venison for beef which he took to the Duncans. Give him time enough, Chip thought, and he could probably find where Pete had cached the hides of the Flying U yearling which the "wolves" had killed. He would be willing to bet all he owned that Pete himself was the "wolf." The hides, of course, were where they could be discovered when the trap was sprung; close to the Duncan camp, no doubt, with Pete involved as the easy-going accomplice after the fact. State's witness? Sure! He could swear that he had seen fresh slaughtered beef, had seen the Duncan boys cook it, had helped them eat it. He wouldn't know, of course, just where it had come from, and he would be surprised to learn that the hides when found did not bear the Duncan brand.

That much was perfectly clear, and the cold-blooded treachery of the plot filled Chip with a rage that would have startled Dunk Whittaker could he have seen it. No use telling Bob and Steve what was brewing, he thought. There was no proof. Anything they said or did now would be used against them. He wished there was some way of knowing where the hides were cached. With them out of the way, the case would fall flat—and for that reason they were well hidden where the Duncan boys would not run across them and spring the trap prematurely.

He wished too that he knew where the killing would come in. That would be Bob; maybe shot when the arrest was made. The vindictiveness of Dunk Whittaker, planning a crime like that to revenge himself for a few well-chosen curses, made Chip shiver. All the more reason, he told himself, why he must stop the thing right now before the plan had ripened into action. It would be too late, then.

There was so much he needed to know; so much he

could only guess at. That killing wasn't necessary at all. Dunk could break Bob and Steve without that. All he had to do was sic the sheriff onto them at the right time and let the law take its course—assisted by Pete Riser's perjured evidence.

He had to make sure Pete was the man, though. It was a cinch that Pete was the fellow he had seen pulling out of town. Chunky brown horse branded D Bar, man with fur cap and sourdough coat—that all tallied right to the dot. But he couldn't swear Pete was the man in the booth talking with Dunk. Let him once get that settled to his satisfaction, and it seemed as though he ought to be able to throw a monkey wrench into their plot. Only, he wanted to do more than that and get them stopped before they started.

It did not take him long to settle one point in his mind. Pete Riser was in camp, overhauling a bunch of traps and greasing them before he stowed them away for the summer. He had his fur cap cocked back on the peak of his head that warm afternoon, and his little eyes squinted suspiciously as Chip rode up at an easy fox-trot. His glance darted to the brand and learned nothing, because Chip was riding his own horse, Mike, with his own private brand on. Pete's eyes swung again to the rider and sized up the whole slim length of him, from high dimpled hatcrown to handmade riding boots resting negligently in the stirrups.

Chip looked him over with unsmiling scrutiny. "You the fellow they call Pete Riser?"

Pete's upper lip lifted and tightened across big yellow teeth. "Well, if I am, that's nothin' to you, is it?"

That whining voice with its undernote of complaint! It sent Chip's shoulders back, stiffened his neck. The man in the booth—he would swear to that in court, if he had to do it. He hoped it wouldn't come to that. Already a plan was taking shape in his mind.

"Ah, don't be so damned suspicious," he admonished crisply and swung down from the saddle. "You're waiting for a message from Dunk Whittaker, aren't you?"

With a grunt of surprise, Pete stepped away from his pile of traps. "Whit never sent yuh—comin' at me like that, without the right sign—" He stopped himself abruptly. "Who the hell are you?"

"Oh, come off your perch—you and your signs!" Chip's thoughts raced like hounds on a hot scent. *Whit,* eh? No one in the country ever called Dunk Whittaker that, so far as he had ever heard. That came from some other time and place, when Dunk and this wolfer had known each other.

He looked at Pete more sharply. "It's enough that I know you're down here waiting till the killing is pulled off."

"K-killin'?" Pete's grimy face went yellow as old suet. "There wasn't s'posed—" Again he stopped as if an unseen hand had slapped him on the mouth.

"Wasn't supposed to be any killing? What did you think it was going to be? A taffy pull or something?" Chip stood watching Pete's slack jaw stiffen. "You swallowed the bait, didn't you? 'Just a matter of form! Just a state's witness!'" His laugh was a lash on Pete's self-esteem. "Just the goat, that's all."

"I dunno what you're talkin' about." Color surged into Pete's face, as his wits and his courage came back. "Say, you straddle yore cayuse and git to hell outa here!" His voice was suddenly loud, blustering. "Come here talkin' through your hat about Whit and some damned killin' I don't know nothin' about—it's all poppycock, I tell yuh. Pull yore freight, or I'll make yuh damned hard to ketch!"

"Yes?" Maddening sarcasm was in Chip's tone. "Well, *you* won't be so hard to catch, if you let them rope you in on this frame-up. It won't be any matter of form, either. The way they'll railroad you to the gallows won't be slow."

"Say, you think you're all-fired sharp now, don't yuh?" Pete was falling back on a purely mechanical repartee, stalling for time to think.

Chip looked up from the cigarette he was rolling. "Don't worry about me, old-timer. You're the guy that could certainly use some brains right now, if you had them. What you need is to see how you're being jobbed."

"Aw, you're crazy!" But the wolfer's little eyes had a furtive, worried look. "You git outa here. I don't wanta tell yuh again."

"Then don't." Chip licked down his cigarette and twisted the ends. "I just rode over from the Duncan place," he added meaningly.

Pete started, gave his tormentor a quick look and pulled himself together with an effort. "What the hell difference does that make?"

"Plenty, don't you think?"

"I don't think nothin' about it. What's them beef-stealin' Duncans been tellin' yuh?"

"Nothing I didn't know. Where you've cached the hides—"

"Hunh?" The sound was jarred from Pete before he could catch his mental balance. "What hides?"

"The hides of the Flying U beef you killed. You know what I mean, well enough. Remember, Pete, it was *you* beefed those critters, and you that packed the meat in to the Duncans. You've been played for a sucker and don't know it."

"Aw, rats!"

Chip shrugged and let it go at that. He had Pete worried, he could see that; worried and dangerous. But Pete wasn't giving himself away except with his eyes. And suddenly Chip understood why Dunk Whittaker had chosen this trapper and wolfer to help him get the Duncans so deep in trouble they would have to let their ranch go for next to nothing. Pete Riser was something more than a wolfer. Dunk must know him pretty well—well enough to trust him with dangerous business. Trusted,—or had some hold on Pete.

That was it, probably. Dunk would always hold the joker, you could bet on that. Pete Riser was pretty tough, by the look of him. If Dunk could snap the whip and make Pete roll over and play dead dog, then it was a cinch he had a stranglehold. Murder, maybe—Pete certainly looked capable of it, and it would take something like that to make Dunk safe in trusting him to plant the evidence down here.

He tried a shot in the dark. "I happen to know Dunk

has got the deadwood on you for that—" A gleam in Pete's eyes warned him just in time. His hand smacked down on the butt of his gun and Pete's fingers fell away from the skinning knife in his belt.

"Better not," Chip said smoothly. "Knife me now and you jam Dunk Whittaker's plans—and what would he do to you then?"

Pete's fingers twitched at his side. "Say, you know too damn much for your own good," he snarled. "Who are yuh? If Whit sent yuh down here, why the hell don't yuh say so?" His eyes squinted half-shut. A panicky kind of fury swept into his crafty face, pulling his lips back from snaggy teeth. "Say, by—, if you've come down in here to spy on me, I'll—"

"Well, you'll do what?"

For answer, Pete lunged forward, quick and deadly as the wolves he trapped. He caught Chip off his guard, expecting nothing worse than threats. Landing fair, his fist would have dropped any man in his tracks, but as it happened, Chip ducked almost soon enough and one knuckle merely raked the skin from a lean brown cheek as the fist shot past. And before there was another, Chip smashed a blow on Pete's ear. Yellow teeth bared, Pete closed in, hooked a leg under Chip's knee and tried to throw him.

But Chip had not lived with Jim Whitmore's rambunctious Happy Family for three years and more without learning to take care of himself in any kind of a scrap. The thing he dreaded most was that knife, but Pete made no attempt to draw it. Perhaps he feared Dunk too much, though it would be dangerous to bank on that. Chip squirmed loose, struck and stepped back, stepped in and landed another that somehow failed to connect.

He had tried to give a knockout blow, but Pete was too wary. A slippery, shifting fighter, giving a blow and darting back out of reach, rushing in again to a clinch and tearing loose before Chip had fairly got hold of him. Also he was not finicky about mayhem, and clamped his stained teeth down on a hand. But Chip retaliated by digging his other thumb deep into Pete's windpipe until the mean little eyes popped and the teeth let go in a hurry, leaving their ugly imprint on skin and flesh.

After that Chip forgot all the rules except one, which had to do with self-preservation. His long-shanked spurs bothered him until he discovered that Pete wore cowhide shoes, whereupon he roweled Pete's shins unmercifully whenever he got close enough. He had the satisfaction of making Pete yelp and try to protect himself there, forgetting his guard. Then a lucky drive of Chip's fist sent Pete down in a clutter of rough cobblestones, where he lay slack, blood trickling from his nose and a cut lip puffed double its normal size.

He was not a pretty sight. His legs sprawled wide, toes turned outward. Below his knees his overalls were slashed and stained with blood from his scratched shins. But he was alive, as Chip made certain before he limped off to where Mike stood impatiently pawing a furrow with one front foot but never stirring from his tracks or dragging the long reins dropped to the ground.

As he climbed the dim trail up along the side of the hill across from Pete's cabin, Chip rode with his face turned over his shoulder, watching with a secret uneasiness the inert figure lying in the shallow wash. Suddenly he heaved a sigh of relief. The vanquished wolfer was struggling to sit up, weaving like a drunken man and feeling around among the rocks for his fur cap.

"I guess that'll hold him for awhile, the damned Judas," Chip muttered to himself, and touched Mike with the spurs that had ravelings of blue denim tangled in the rowels.

CHAPTER FIVE
CHIP TRAILS A WOLF

As he approached the place where the trail forked, a little-used branch leading off into the Duncan basin, Chip pulled his horse down to a loitering walk while he tried to make up his mind. Maybe he ought to warn Bob and Steve after all; put them on their guard. The trouble was, he'd have to be so vague they wouldn't take him seriously. It wasn't as if he had anything definite to go on. They'd ask him a lot of questions he couldn't answer and end by doing nothing about it.

When he came right down to facts, he had to admit that he was doing a lot of guessing. Dunk and Pete Riser were plotting against someone—that much he could swear to. But he couldn't swear it was the Duncans they had in mind. He had a hunch and he had satisfied himself that it was a good one. Pete had all but admitted it. But even if Bob or the ironical Steve took his suspicions seriously, what could they do about it? Not a darned thing until the plotters made a move, and then it would probably be too late. He couldn't help remembering now that a man's personal opinion isn't worth much when it is put to the test. Circumstances, facts, actions are what count in the eyes of the law.

Still, it seemed as though Bob and Steve ought to know. He pulled his eyebrows together and chewed a corner of his lip, even reined Mike into the Duncan trail and rode down it and rode slowly along it for a quarter of a mile, trying to make up his mind whether to tell them or not. Then abruptly he reined Mike out of the trail and cut across through brush and rocks toward the main road which led out of the Badlands to the wind-swept world beyond.

Actions were better than words, he told himself. He was going to try a little action. He rather thought it would work.

It was farther and rougher across that stretch of barren flat than he would have believed. A deep, straight-walled dry wash barred his way before he had covered half the distance, and he was obliged to ride up around the head of it before he could cross, which brought him into a nest of narrow little ridges like spread fingers at rest, over which he must climb as best he might. He was tempted to turn back and go around the way he had come, but from the top of each ridge he could see the white limestone cliff that marked the main trail before him. So he kept on.

An odd thing happened; odd because of that lonely place where human beings could be counted on one hand with a finger or two left over. When he finally did come out of a deep gully into the trail, he rode into a white smother of dust with no wind to lift it from the road. Someone had passed along that road within two or three minutes of his arrival, though at first he could not tell in which direction. Later he saw hoofprints pointing ahead of him, and saw too that whoever it was had ridden in haste, as the smothery dust and the length of his horse's stride gave proof.

The Duncan boys had not mentioned riding out of the hills that day or any time soon, but there was a man who no doubt was very anxious to get somewhere in a hurry. And while he had not appeared to be in any condition to ride when Chip last saw him, a good half hour had been wasted on that cut-off. Long enough for Pete Riser to saddle a horse and ride this far.

A vicious devil! The kind that would follow and shoot a man in the back, if he thought he could get away with it. Chip was just as well pleased to have Pete ahead of him, since they were going the same way. With tight mouth he sent Mike cautiously forward, slowing on the sharp turns and peering ahead, half suspecting a trap.

He wanted no more trouble just now. If it were Pete—and he was sure of it—he was probably on his way to see Dunk. Once those two got together, the fur would certainly fly somewhere. No use telling the Duncans, no use riding back to the ranch and telling J. G. what his fine partner was up to. No one would believe that the dignified banker from Helena would stoop to plot against a couple of poor ranchers, whose only crime was their possession of a few hundred acres of desirable land. Even if they did believe that, they would laugh at the idea of his taking a fellow like Pete Riser into his confidence. They'd just give him the laugh—and Chip had a horror of ridicule. Even Weary had accused him of mixing his drinks and not hearing straight.

But he had heard straight and he had proved it to his own satisfaction that day. If Dunk went ahead, he had the money and the power to put it over. Steve and Bob wouldn't be the first honest ranchers railroaded to the penitentiary on faked evidence of rustling. It would be an ugly mark against the Flying U—and the worst of it was, J. G. and his outfit would be blamed for it all. No one would believe the high-headed banker had anything to do with it.

The whole Flying U outfit would get a black eye—and after all, that was what most worried Chip Bennett. He had a fierce, inarticulate jealousy for the good name of his outfit; a fighting loyalty which would not count the cost, but throw itself wholeheartedly into the defence of Jim Whitmore's honor. If Dunk went through with it—But he wouldn't. He shouldn't. Not if he had every renegade in the country under his thumb, ready to swear Bob and Steve Duncan into jail; or ready to dry gulch them as Chip was afraid might happen.

Pete Riser or another, the horseman ahead rode at top speed. Trying to make up that lost half-hour, Chip told himself with a sardonic twist of his lips. What would Pete say if he knew who was coming behind him? Chip was young enough to grin at the joke. He was tempted to ride up close and let out a yell, just to see what Pete would do. But it was a fleeting impulse, gone as quickly as it came. He had too much on his mind to waste time.

The last ridge was crossed, the last winding canyon lay behind them. The dust of the rider in the lead billowed out into the road and was whipped aside as the horseman turned north. Half a mile away he showed as a bobbing black object against the brown ribbon of road, still pounding along at a fast lope and apparently never looking behind him.

Chip's own small dust-cloud kept pace with Mike's steady gallop. Clear to the skyline three or four miles away there was no dust save those two swift-moving clouds. So they galloped steadily along. A mile ahead, the road to Flying II coulee slid around behind a hill. Pete Riser galloped past the turn-off, never slackening his speed. Chip came loping up to the spot, thought swiftly whether he should go home, as his boss expected him to do, or keep on Pete's trail.

A momentous decision, that. He made it with a lift of his shoulders and no inner warning of how much hung in the balance as he spurred a disappointed Mike past the familiar rutty trail.

The road swung westward there, and for the first time he noticed that the sun was ready to drop behind the high level bench that rose beyond Dry Lake. Far ahead of him, the small gray cloud moving along the ground caught rose tints, but even his artist soul saw no beauty there. It merely meant that Pete Riser was gaining on him, would reach Dry Lake minutes ahead of him.

Stubborn lines settled around Chip's mouth and he lifted Mike into a longer stride. There were men in that new cow town who might be in on the plot—for what money there would be in it for them. If Pete were hurrying to see someone in town, Chip wanted to know who that man was.

With that thought, he pushed in closer as the twilight deepened and rode into town a scant hundred yards behind the man he was following. He was in time to see Pete's horse disappearing into the livery stable, and he pulled up in the shadow of the stable and swung off, standing out of sight behind his horse.

Pete came out and started across the street. He was not wearing his fur cap now, but a soft felt hat; slicked up for high-toned company, Chip decided, and wondered if Pete were going to call on a girl. Not with the marks he bore, however. He must be headed somewhere else—probably to Helena.

Then Squint came into the doorway and called after him, "You got lots uh time. She's late a couple of hours."

Chip led his horse into the stable on the heels of the departing hostler. "Say, Squint, can you kinda lose this cayuse of mine in a corner stall till I come after him?"

"Sure! Sure!" Squint gave him a knowing grin. " 'Fraid the gal's father might go on the warpath, hunh? Or mebby you're cuttin' out some other feller!"

"Suit yourself. Both, maybe. Only remember, this horse isn't here till I come after him myself." He pulled off his overcoat and tied it to the saddle. "Wasn't that Pete Riser that rode in ahead of me?"

"Yeah, that was him. Hope he ain't the feller you're cuttin' in on, Chip. There's a bad actor—and I ain't foolin'. He's got business up the line, I guess. He was askin' about the up train and he left his horse here overnight." Squint spat into a pile of straw. "How'd a box stall do yuh? I got one."

"All right. It's no life-and-death matter, but I thought maybe some of the boys might be in. If they come, don't let them run any whizzer on you and take my horse back to the ranch. That's all."

"Oh." Squint looked slightly crestfallen. "That's what it is; some devilment amongst you Flyin' U fellers. All right, I don't turn 'im over to nobody but you."

Having sufficiently diverted Squint's mind, which lived on small gossip, Chip drifted out into the dusk.

CHAPTER SIX
A LITTLE HEADWORK

It wasn't long now until train time. Pete Riser had already disappeared into the darkness, headed in the general direction of the little depot that squatted opposite the stockyards behind the store. Chip sighed with relief. It certainly had been a long watch, standing guard outside the saloon until Pete showed himself.

Ham and eggs and hot biscuits had helped, though he had been so busy watching every man who stepped out of the saloon next door that he couldn't really enjoy the meal.

With Pete out of the way, he now pushed in through the swinging doors, sending sharp glances this way and that to see who was there and whether they were observing him. Embarrassment darkened his face, pulled his eyebrows together, as he walked straight up to the bar, turning so that his back was toward the room. Rusty Brown's jovial greeting he answered with an upward tilt of his chin, beckoning the proprietor to him.

With a purely mechanical movement, Rusty reached for his towel and wiped his way down the bar to Chip's dark-coated elbow. He paused there, polishing an imaginary stain, cocking an ear expectantly and watching under his eyebrows lest someone blunder too close. A cautious, reliable man was Rusty, quick to understand when a man wanted privacy.

Chip squared his shoulders, snapped out his errand in the first sentence as if he wanted to say it and get it over with.

"I'd like to borrow fifty dollars, Rusty. I can give you an order on the Flying U—I've got it coming."

Rusty shot him a sidelong glance that registered in Chip's very toes, but his hesitation stopped short of reluctance. One of the Flying U boys—that meant pretty dependable. They weren't the borrowing kind, either.

"Why, sure, Chip." And he muttered without moving

his lips, "In a jam? Anything I can do—"

"No, thanks. Just an unforeseen emergency. Only, if any of the boys should happen along, I'd just as soon—"

"Sure. Your business is your business. I never built up my business by shootin' off my face. Anything to drink?"

"Yes, a highball," said Chip, who thought he might need a little Dutch courage for what he had in mind.

Rusty showed a caution that would have done credit to a far more vital cause. The way he slipped three gold pieces out of his till when he made change for a dollar, and the way he slid the money into Chip's hand under cover of the ubiquitous towel, lifted that young man's spirits.

"That enough? You can have more."

"Plenty. Thanks, Rusty. If you want an order on—"

"Aw, forget it. Your word's good enough, Chip."

"Well, thanks." It seemed a weak way of expressing his appreciation, but three thirsty cowpunchers were nearing the bar and Rusty had already turned to meet them. Chip went out, promising himself that he'd carry a roll after this. A fellow never knew when he might need money, and it certainly was damned awkward to be caught without it. Who'd ever have thought, when he stepped into the saddle to ride down to the Duncan place, that he'd be needing money for train travel that night?

His actions in the next half-hour were as cautious as if he were planning to rob a bank. Ordinarily he would have crossed the tracks and taken the smooth cinder path up along the other side to the depot platform end, but tonight he walked between freight cars and the stockyard fence until he came opposite the depot, and then he stood there between two cars, watching the lighted space outside the windows straight across from him. Four or five men loitered there, but Pete Riser was not one of them. He peered into the shadows where freight was piled, watching for a lurking figure to move and betray its presence. There was nothing. The ticket window was open, but no one was in the waiting room and the operator was busy at his table with a green shade over his eyes.

A livery rig rattled up and swung in an arc behind the depot, coming to a stand behind the baggage-and-express room. Squint joined the group, a stiff-crowned cap with EXPRESS across the front tilted importantly over his nose. His arrival was proof that the delayed train would soon be in. He stared toward the north, tilted a silver watch out of his pocket, gave it the negligent glance of a trainman, sent another one to the clock in the office and spat out over the edge of the platform.

"She oughta be showin' around the butte most any minute now," he remarked to the group, as one who had special information on the subject.

The butte stood ten miles up the track toward Havre. That meant twelve or fifteen minutes in which to locate Pete. Chip backed, crouching under the car couplings, and ran on his toes down along the stockyard fence to the corner, crossed the tracks there in the dark and walked back toward the depot. He might have been any man taking the short cut up from town to meet the train; he might, that is, until he reached the ramp at the platform end, and after that anyone who noticed him would have wondered what he was up to.

The men farther along the platform were busily haw-hawing over some questionable joke, however, and did not see him. Chip made sure of that while he paused to roll a cigarette, which he dropped when he saw he was safe from observation. He went then to Squint's team, where they stood in the dark behind the depot, and patted shoulders and fussed with the harness while he scrutinized every inch of that shadowed back wall.

No luck. Pete wouldn't be there, anyway. He'd be up at the north end, where no one would have occasion to go, and where he could board the train unseen; though why he should be so scared of having folks see him was a mystery, except that it was proof that there was something devilish brewing. Pete was high-tailing it to Helena to see Dunk Whittaker. At least, that was his intention.

Silent as a cat stalking a ground sparrow, Chip moved along the wall to the corner. There he stopped and listened. At first there was nothing, then he heard a faint shuffling sound, as if someone were leaning against the building and had just changed his position. It was Pete, all right. Chip would have bet money on that. He was standing close to the corner, so if anyone came up to the end of the platform, he could duck around out of sight.

No one came. Pete did not move again, nor did Chip, for some minutes.

Far off across the prairie a star rose suddenly, low down against the dim horizon to the north, where one would not expect a star to rise. From the ground where he stood that pinpoint of light looked too high to be the headlight, until Chip remembered that the train was now at the head of a long downgrade. The gleam grew, crawled slowly to the eastward and disappeared for a full half-minute. When it showed again it was bigger, a bright little moon looking just ready to slip back over the hill. A faint pulse of sound began to beat upon the night. It was the train, all right, thundering over the prairie, trying to make up lost time.

A pulse began to hammer in Chip's throat just under the point of his jaw. Holding his breath lest it betray him somehow, he inched closer to the corner. Almost as if aware of his presence, the man against the north wall moved restlessly, edging toward the front. Still Chip waited, but his gun was in his hand and his teeth were clamped so hard together that his jaw muscles bulged. His eyes never left that growing light. The faint whistle as it cut through the thrumming tingled his nerves.

Pete would be watching that light just as intently. He wouldn't be thinking that someone might slip around the corner—Chip did it, walking on his toes, afraid the gravel might crunch under his tread. Against the light filtering out along the platform, he could see Pete standing out a few inches from the wall, his head turned, watching the train sweeping in around the wide curve of Lonesome Prairie's bold rocky slope. The thrumming had grown to a subdued roar. The headlight was a blazing ball down by the water tank.

Chip dared wait no longer. There came the swift and noiseless rush of his feet, the plop of his gun barrel crashing down upon soft felt. Pete crumpled up like something melting in a sudden blast of heat. When the headlight rushed up seconds later to paint that north wall with a passing brilliance, it showed what looked to be a long bundle of something rolled against the depot. It also swept the platform and lighted the moving figures there, but it did not shine upon young Chip Bennett.

When the engine had slowed to a panting halt down by the corner of the stockyard, a tall young cowpuncher stepped unhurriedly upon the ramp beside the baggage car. He strolled up to the level of the platform, stood there smoking a cigarette until the conductor swung his lantern and chanted "A-a-ll *abo-oard?*" and the wheels began to turn. Then, as if he were merely following the impulse of that moment, he tossed away his cigarette, stepped forward and caught the handrail at the front end of the smoking car.

An odd misgiving came to plague him as he walked down the aisle, looking for an empty seat. He thought, "My Lord, what if that wasn't Pete Riser I crowned?"

CHAPTER SEVEN
CHIP TURNS A DEAL

As he stepped down from the train in Helena, Chip stopped as if a flung noose had settled and jerked him backwards. With that premonitory prickling at the nape of his neck, his hair lifted in the battle sign. For down by the rear end of the train he had just left, Pete Riser was walking out into the street, evidently headed for a dingy-looking eating house just across the way. He looked slightly rumpled and he wore his hat perched at an odd angle on the back of his head, but there was no mistaking that big hulking figure. It was Pete, without a doubt.

Breakfast had been uppermost in Chip's thoughts a moment before, but while he watched Pete open the restaurant door and disappear inside, all desire for food was swept away by this fresh urgency. Pete's appetite should require half an hour—more, probably, since it was about halfway between breakfast time and noon, and he would have to order from the short-order card. With luck, he might be there some little time.

With the old stubborn look around his mouth, Chip waved a rusty-looking hack in to the curb and crawled in. "Take me to the Helena State Bank, *pronto*," he ordered curtly. And although the hackman failed to get the speed out of his team that Chip would have gotten, they arrived just as the plate-glass door swung open to let the first customer inside.

Chip was the second. He made rather a striking picture in that marble-and-onyx grandeur with his big Stetson cocked over his right eyebrow and his silver spurs making a musical burring sound on the checkerboard floor. High-heeled boots gave him a stilted walk that suggested arrogance, and his fringed leather chaps made his body look slimmer. Just why he had buckled

48

on his spurs in the hack he could not have told, but he felt more at home with them jingling at his heels as he went into action.

He was not thinking about his appearance, however. Eyes that turned his way met his aloof, straight glance and slid off embarrassed until he was past and they could stare all they pleased—for Helena, as you should know, was a nice little city most interested in mines, and cowboys were worth a second glance.

So he burred uncompromisingly up to the nearest window, which chanced to be marked "NOTES", and shifted his hat a little so that it would not scrape the grill when he bent to look in. "I want to see Mr. Whittaker. You may tell him I'm from the Flying U." And since he most certainly looked it, the gentle old man behind the grill smiled companionably—and a bit enviously as well—and pointed toward Dunk's office. So presently Chip stood in a room of somber elegance and stared across a wide mahogany desk at the man he had taken some trouble to see.

"Well! Well!" Dunk Whittaker leaned back in his revolving chair, rocking it gently while he regarded his caller with the half-amused and wholly tolerant smile which for some reason always made Chip want to slap his face. "Our gay buckaroo gallops off to see the bright lights! And what can I do for you? Advance a month's pay, or tell the judge what a good boy you are?"

Probably he merely wanted to be friendly and tried to imitate the Happy Family's rough joshing, but his tone, his smile and the words he spoke combined to give the last sharp impetus to Chip's purpose and mood.

"What can you do? You can keep your paws spread out on that blotter, away from all your fancy little call buttons. And you can keep your mouth shut and your ears wide open, because I'm here to talk turkey and I'm talking fast."

Dunk's black eyes narrowed at the gun in Chip's hand. He looked like a boy watching sleight-of-hand tricks, wondering how that gun got there without his seeing it drawn. His fingers twitched on the clean blue blotter that covered a third of his desk, but his voice was controlled, faintly contemptuous under its manifest astonishment.

"Are you crazy, or just drunk?"

"Neither one. Just playing safe. I was down talking with Pete Riser yesterday—hold still, there! Pete," he said with cold preciseness, "has got cold feet on that nice little scheme you've cooked up for the Duncan boys. He isn't a damned bit anxious to be hauled into jail and trust you to get him out again. He's scared as a trapped coyote right now. And," he added, with a twist of his lips to point the grim humor he saw in the situation, "if I'm not badly mistaken, he'll come stampeding in here about the next thing you know, hollering his head off."

"Why, the dirty, double-crossing—" Dunk's mouth shut like a trap, though not quite soon enough.

Chip's eyes betrayed a certain relief. "Yes, exactly. And I don't give a tinker's damn how you two settle your argument. You have the deadwood on Pete, of course, or you never would have put him down there to plant evidence against Bob and Steve Duncan. I'm not concerned with that—"

"What are you after, then? Is this blackmail?" Dunk's swarthy skin was two shades darker than normal. His eyes held venom.

"Well, call it what you like. The Duncan boys made you a price on their ranch and it wasn't any too much; you just got pinch-gutted and thought you'd rather frame them into the pen or force them to give you their place for a song. You'd ruin a couple of good boys to save a few thousand dollars, you dirty skunk."

"Pete Riser's word isn't worth a thing. Why, he's—"

"Never mind Pete. You've got a job of work to do and I want you to get at it. Make out a deed to the Duncan ranch on our creek and put it in escrow with the money—ten thousand dollars is what they want for it. Fix up that escrow with that bank right across the street. The First National. I'll see to it that the boys sign the deed, all right. Put the full amount down, cash to be paid on delivery. You—"

"I'll see you in hell first!"

"Oh, no, you won't. You might be looking for me, all right, but I don't expect to arrive for quite awhile yet. You go ahead and fix up those papers. I've got you over a barrel, Dunk. I know all about that frame-up. All about what Pete was supposed to do—and the killing—"

"He's a damned liar if he says—"

"Well, you want to bear in mind that I happened to hear you talking in at Rusty Brown's saloon—back in

51

that booth, remember? I'd be the star witness against you, Dunk. Better get busy with that deed."

"That," said Dunk sullenly, "will take a little time."

"Half an hour, maybe. I got all that stuff in school, as it happens. You could do it a lot quicker at a pinch. If you haven't got the description, I can tell you just how that land lies." He caught his lip between his teeth, studying.

"Call in your clerk. I'm not alone on this. Weary's line-riding for me today, so if you try any funny business, you'll be the sorriest crook that ever warmed an office chair. I'll put up my gun—but remember this, you blinkety-blink blank-blank-blank, I'm doing this for J. G.—to keep his name from being dragged through the mud of a court trial—and I'm prepared to go the limit. If I have to shoot you and a few more just like yuh, I'll sure do it. So would any of the boys, far as that goes. By going ahead and buying that ranch at a fair price, you'll save J. G. a lot of grief and the thing ends right there, far as I'm concerned. That's all. Get him in here and see you don't stick any flaws in the title, or I'll be right on top of you with a flock of bullets—" Chip suddenly wanted to laugh, though he was not in the least amused. Dunk spoke a sentence through his teeth.

"Well, that's all right. Weary and I are used to being cussed. Another thing, while we're alone. You play straight from now on; straight with the nesters and with J. G. All this freeze-out business has got to stop. J. G. don't like it and us boys don't like it. You can get rich fast enough and do it honest. Square up this Duncan deal, and J. G. won't ever need to know a word about it."

"Well, put up that gun," snarled Dunk, "and let me get this thing over with. I have an appointment—You win your little game, since I'm not disposed to let you stir up a lot of trouble. But I shall make it my business to settle with you and Pete Riser later. Make no mistake about that."

"All right, don't you make any, either." Chip sat down where he could command both doors and the desk, and although his gun was back in its holster, his hand was not far from it while he waited. A baldheaded clerk came in soft-footed, bowed meekly aver the orders he received, went out and returned with a folder of legal-looking papers. Apparently the Duncan deed was already drawn up and ready to sign. Without a word, Dunk signed two documents, pushing them across the desk for Chip's inspection.

With his left hand and only half his gaze, Chip took the papers and read every word. "You better change that 'Ten dollars and other valuable considerations' to ten thousand. And you've got the description wrong in one place," he said. "The buildings stand on the southeast quarter of the west half of Section Four. You've got it the southeast quarter. Aside from that, it's fine."

And Dunk Whittaker, president of the Helena State Bank, scowled blacker than ever and sent the papers back for corrections.

When the clerk returned, he leaned and spoke close to his employer's ear: "A man who gives his name as

53

Peter M. Riser would like to see you on urgent business."

"I'll see him next."

Dunk's voice promised so much more than he realized that Chip's mouth curved in a boyish grin. His eyes twinkled all through the rest of the interview, though Dunk was too preoccupied to notice.

"I'll go along with this fellow to the other bank—and see to it he gets across the street safe with all that money," Chip announced laconically, standing up when the bald-headed clerk returned for the last time with the cash, which this strange young cowboy had insisted upon, instead of the customary cashier's check. And he nearly grinned again when he saw how the clerk eyed that gun in its holster, and how he edged out of the office ahead of his escort and forgot to get his hat.

In the pillared main lobby, Chip swerved aside and gathered in Pete Riser, who was leaning against a high counter with his legs crossed. "You don't want to see anybody in here, Pete. You better come along with me. I've got something to show yuh that'll sure bug your eyes out."

The blank look of amazement on Pete Riser's battered countenance changed swiftly to fear, his eyes turning toward the door of Dunk's office and back again, as he unwound his legs and took his elbows off the counter. "Wha—how the hell did you—?" Then he caught a certain look in Chip's eyes and went out into the street behind the bald-headed clerk who was not at all sure this was not a holdup and required the attention of the police.

But nothing happened that would cause a passer-by to stop and look again. Indeed, the transaction became pure humdrum routine. The escrow clerk in the bank across the street must have wondered why the tall young cowboy and the other nondescript individual who had been in a fight had tagged along to watch the mere details of the business. His eyes followed them to the door while the next customer waited, but he saw nothing at all out of the way.

On the sidewalk Chip paused, his glance going to a restaurant sign two doors down the street. He turned to Pete Riser. "Go on and see Dunk now, if you've got the nerve," he advised succinctly. "But if I was you, I'd high-tail it outa the country. That paper you saw back in there was a deed to the Duncan ranch that I'm taking down for the boys to sign, and that money you saw is theirs the minute they turn over the deed. Looks like you're out of a job, old-timer."

"Not till I'm square with you, I ain't," Pete retorted, with a flash of spirit.

"Well, let me tell you something. Poke your long nose into Flying U country again and you won't need any job,—never, no more. Now drift. Get outa my sight."

Until Pete had disappeared around a corner, Chip stood there watching. Then, with a long sigh of thankfulness, he turned into the restaurant for his belated breakfast.

CHAPTER EIGHT

CROSS-PURPOSES

Because his train had been delayed six hours by a freight wreck forty miles out of Dry Lake, it was almost noon when Chip rode in to the Duncan camp. He clattered down the last little slope and set Mike up with a flourish before the two brothers, who were at work on a new corral. With their deed safely buttoned within his coat, a man-sized hunger growling in his stomach and the glow of well-doing warming the cockles of his heart, he looked exactly what he was—a young man proud of himself and tickled with the good news he had brought.

Being what he was, he would have denied that he was excited. But he would have grinned over his denial, just as he did when he swung off beside the two and wanted to know why they didn't have dinner ready, and what was the idea of starving a man to death.

"Well, my Lord!" Steve ejaculated, grinning in sympathy. "Day before yestiddy, you rode off when we was beggin' yuh to stay for another meal, and here today you come foggin' into camp beefin' around because your dinner ain't settin' on the table waitin' for yuh! Where the hell yuh been, to git so hungry?"

While he loosened the latigo and pulled off the saddle, laying it on its side against the fence, Chip flung amazing words over his shoulder. "I've been to

56

Helena, if anybody should ask yuh—which I hope they won't. Had breakfast on the train and I'm so hungry right now I could eat a little man off his horse. Didn't want to stop in Dry Lake for a meal—didn't want anyone to peddle the news to the Flying U."

"Well, I'll be switched! You sure cut a wide circle, boy. Come on up to the house. Ain't nothing to do but warm up the coffee and open a can or two of corn. I got a lot of stuff cooked up ahead." Bob stood with his hands on his hips, watching while Steve brought a forkful of hay for Mike, then led the way along the footpath to the cabin.

"What took yuh off to Helena in such a damn hurry?" he asked, half turning toward Chip. "If it's any of my business," he amended.

"It certainly is your business," Chip grinned, aching to tell it. "Wait till we get inside and I'll show you something that'll make your hair curl. Come on, Steve—that darned cayuse has been eating his head off in Squint's stable since Sunday. Do him good to eat post hay for awhile."

Steve stood the fork against the fence well away from the horse's heels. "What's eatin' on yuh, Chip? You act plumb locoed."

Chip stalked on ahead, making no reply to that. As a rule, he kept his feelings pretty much to himself, and it occurred to him now that maybe he was making something of a show of himself. The Duncans must think he was crazy, all right, acting like a fool kid.

Inside the cabin he therefore stated his errand in few words—or tried to. It was no use. With that glow of triumph running warm in his blood, he couldn't just hand over the deed and let it go at that. He had to explain exactly how and why the miracle had been accomplished, and because he was a modest young man who never had learned to sing his own praises, it took time to get the full story from him.

Before they got up from the table to go about their work again, the afternoon was more than half gone. "You stay all night," Bob urged, his hand clamped down on Chip's shoulder. "My Lord, I don't know how ever to thank yuh enough, kid. Me and Steve boosted the price up to ten thousand because we figured we'd have to come down anyway—that skunk is such a tight-wad in any kinda deal—and if we started high, we could let the son of a gun jew us down and still get a fair price. Six or seven thousand is about what she's worth. There's a lot of doby on that east—"

"I know what's on every foot of that land, Bob. You asked ten thousand and that's what you got. Let 'er ride."

"Well," Bob insisted, "but we want to give you the difference—"

Chip whirled on him. "Give me money? Not on your life! Say, it was worth a million to take it out of old Dunk. All I ask from you boys is to keep the whole thing under your hats. I wouldn't for the world have J. G. find out what I did to the Flying U bank roll. On the way back, I got to thinking that half that money has to come out of his pocket, probably—though I notice Dunk had the deed made out to himself, personally. I guess he figures on keeping the details from the Old

Man as long as he can. In fact, I more or less made that part of the bargain,—that J. G. wouldn't know anything about the dirty work Dunk was framing."

"He oughta be booted off the ranch the minute he steps on it," Steve exclaimed vindictively. "Don't seem right to me, not to let J. G. know what kinda pardner he's got."

"Oh, Dunk's going to be damn careful after this," Chip declared, getting up and reaching for his hat. "I certainly threw it into him plenty strong that the outfit was going to keep a weather eye on his activities from now on.

"Well, I'll have to be drifting, or old J. G.'ll be sending out the mess wagon to round me up. I never told anyone where I was going—"

"Yeah, and Weary was over here yesterday looking for you," Bob tardily informed him. "All I could tell him was that you left right after dinner Sunday, and far as I knew you was hittin' the high spots for home."

"Which," said Chip, "I'm doing right now, if anybody comes around inquiring for me. But keep what I've told you behind your teeth, remember."

"Well," Bob suddenly decided, "You wait till I git into my war togs and I'll ride with yuh as far as the turn-off. And another thing, you'll have to put your John Henry on this-here deed. Both copies. It calls for a witness when we sign, and if we don't do it up brown and accordin' to Hoyle, that high-collared polecat is liable to crawfish on the deal."

"That's right, Chip," Steve for once agreed with his brother. "We want your name on 'er, just to kinda remind old Dunk he can't git away with nothin' around where you're at."

That idea tickled Chip immensely. With much hilarity the three signed the two copies of the paper, which was worth exactly ten thousand dollars in cash, Chip writing his name with extra curls on his capitals and a final flourish of scrolls which only his artist's hand could accomplish. Dunk would know exactly what he meant by that flamboyant signature—he would bet a month's wages on that.

When all was done to their full satisfaction, he lay down on the bunk and slept while Bob brought in a tub of water, heated it on the stove and took a bath, shaved, sat with a dirty dish towel draped around his neck while Steve trimmed his hair, and dressed himself in his "store" clothes. It all took time.

That is why the sun was dipping out of sight beyond the rim of Flying U coulee when Chip loped up to the corral and swung thankfully down from the saddle, still gently exhilarated by the consciousness of a great service rendered to his beloved outfit at some trouble and expense to himself. That it was a secret service added something to the thrill of it and to the assurance that he had made two fine fellows his friends for life. He whistled while he pulled the saddle and bridle off Mike. . . .

And then the sense of something wrong seeped into his happy mood. The sweaty, saddle-marked horses munching hay inside the round-pole corral told of hard riding that day, and the saddled mounts tied outside indicated more riding to come. The Happy Family came straggling from the mess house, wiping last traces of supper from their faces with hasty swipes of shirt-sleeved wrists, staring at him in ominous silence as they strode toward him. Without knowing what was wrong, Chip braced himself mentally. His whistling hushed abruptly in the middle of a bar.

Neck stiff and arms swinging belligerently, J. G. came bow-legging down the trail from his cabin, and the cowboys stepped aside to let him pass. "Where the dawgone hell have you been keepin' yourself all this while?" he bellowed, while he was yet some distance away.

"I rode down to see the Duncan boys. Why?" Chip's face had become a mask of aloofness, which was a way he had of meeting unwarranted censure.

"Down at the Duncans, ay?" J. G. looked on the verge of apoplexy. "Don't yuh try to run any ranniganse on me! You ain't been to the Duncans since Sunday, and I know it."

Chip's neck stiffened. "That's very strange," he said coldly. "It happens that I just came from there."

"And the hull outfit combin' the hills for yuh! Huntin' yuh from Dry Lake to Cow Island! Hold up everything while we hunted the breaks for your damned worthless carcass—and you come lopin' into camp whistlin' like a—a—" he choked "—claimin' you been at Duncans all this time!"

Chip held himself calm. "I didn't say I'd been there all this time. I said I just came from there. As a matter of fact, I rode in to Dry Lake—"

"And that's another lie on the face of it! I sent Happy

61

Jack in to find out, and he come foggin' back and says you ain't been there!"

Chip's eyes swung to Happy Jack, who goggled back at him accusingly. "Chances are he never asked."

"Aw, gwan!" cried Happy. "I did too. I ast Rusty if he'd saw anything of yuh, and he said no, you hadn't showed up in town fer most a week."

Chip bit his lip in chagrin. Rusty was loyal, no doubt of that, and he wouldn't call him a liar now. He turned again to J. G. "Well, what's the crime? Can't a man have business to attend to that is his own personal, private affair?"

"Not when he's s'posed to be workin' for me, he can't. Not and go sneakin' off without a word to anybody, and let the hull outfit waste time huntin' him, thinkin' he's in trouble somewhere. Where you been and what you been doin'? I want the truth now, and I want it dawgone quick!" That J. G. looked upon this youngest member of his Happy Family with the affection an old bachelor gives to the boy he wishes he might call his son only made his anger the more unreasonable now. "Where yuh been? On some damned spree, most likely. You sure look it."

"Have it that way if you like. A guess is all you'll get when you come at me like that. You or any other man." His gaze traveled disdainfully around the group, meeting eyes sharpened with resentful curiosity. That the resentment grew out of their worry over his unaccountable absence combined with the shock of his blithe return just as they were about to start out again and spend another sleepless night searching for him, never once occurred to him.

All the Happy Family wanted was a proper attitude of remorse, with a plausible explanation of the mystery thrown in. All they got was the stone wall of his hurt pride, and it was not to be wondered at if they misread the sardonic twist of his lips, the exasperating twitch of his shoulders that told them all just where they might go.

Complete and disastrous misunderstanding locked the group in angry silence for an appreciable pause. Then J. G. threw back his shoulders, that had begun to stoop in the last year.

"That's all the satisfaction you think this outfit is entitled to, ay? Busy as we are, gettin' ready for roundup—and have to stop the hull works to go combin' the country day an' night for a feller that's supposed to be shot or layin' with his neck broke—"

"That," said Chip with chilling politeness, "is certainly too bad. But I didn't ask or expect any such solicitude on the part of anyone. In fact, I felt quite capable of taking care of myself."

"Did, ay? Kinda forgot there's been a time er two when you was damn glad to see somebuddy show up and keep yuh from bein' kioty bait!"

"Yeah, and you can sure lay and rot next time, fer all I care," Cal Emmett interpolated disgustedly.

J. G. scowled at the interruption. "If this is all you got to say—"

Chip's shoulders lifted again. "Oh, I'll roll my bed— don't worry about that. Since in all the time I've been with the Flying U, I don't seem to have convinced anyone on the ranch that I usually have a pretty fair reason for what I do, it's time I drifted. If you'll make out my time, J. G., I'll remove myself before the outfit loses any more time or sleep over me."

Blank stares, while the burnt bridge crashed before their eyes. Then Jim Whitmore turned on his heel. "All right, if that's the stand yuh take, you can't go too quick to suit me," he made grim retort as he walked away.

"Mamma, but you sure are making seventeen kinds of a fool of yourself, Chip," Weary the peacemaker observed, in a worried tone. "Why don't you go on up and make a clean breast of it with the Old Man? This is no way to act—"

"When I want a lecture, I'll buy a ticket."

"Aw, let the damn fool alone," Cal Emmett growled. "He's been after some girl and he hates to own up to it. I'll bet—"

What he would bet does not particularly matter, except that Chip took it as an insult, stepped away from Mike and knocked Cal down on the flat of his back. But Cal Emmett was a fighter. He was up again like a cat, as the boys backed off in a crude circle to watch the fight.

This was not the first time those two had tangled, though mostly they had fought for the sport of it. They knew all the tricks, and as a rule they tried each one and gave a very entertaining performance. But tonight Chip's hurt was too deep, his mood was too savage for anything but straight slugging. He wanted to beat and to batter. He came in with short jabs and punches, bewildering Cal with the swift deadliness of his attack. He was fighting the whole Happy family, beating down his own bitterness of disappointment. He had been too proud, too happy over the thing he had accomplished single-handed. He had come home victorious, thinking how the bunk house would roar at the story he would have to tell—under the seal of secrecy, to be sure. How they would chortle at the way he had spiked Dunk's guns—

That last half-hour was like a nightmare from which he could not waken. He was smashing Cal Emmett in the face, and then J. G. was there, handing him a fistful of gold pieces and bills and telling him to go. He was saddling Mike and galloping furiously up to the little pasture after his old pack horse Jeff and his three-year-old colt Silver. Then he was folding his blankets, laying them just so on Jeff's pack, being terribly calm and indifferent about it, because the Happy Family stood back in the shadows, watching every move he made. He was swinging into the saddle, reining Mike into the trail that led up over the rim of the hill and out of the coulee, and Jeff and Silver were wheeling in behind him, as they had long ago been trained to do. He was leaving the Flying U without so much as a glance over his shoulder.

Unreal, nightmarish! The last thing on earth he would ever have expected to do. The most grotesquely improbable home-coming he could have imagined. And yet it was happening just like that and he couldn't stop it. All his distraught mind could crystallize into coherent thought was the hope that none of the outfit would ever see or hear of him again.

That night he camped on the edge of Dry Lake, back in the willows alongside the creek that watered the valley. He rode in and paid Rusty Brown the money he owed him, bought enough provisions at the store to last him for a week and more, and by daybreak he was on his way again, riding to the Cow Island crossing of the Missouri River. He rode fast until he was well past the trail that turned off to the Flying U, and he kept to the hollows lest someone should glimpse him and know which direction he was taking.

In a secluded little niche of a coulee he had made use of once before for a hidden camp, he stayed and rested his horses that afternoon and well into the evening, and forded the river by starlight somewhere near midnight. Like a man in fear of capture, his hurt pride drove him forward all the rest of that night and into another hidden camp just after sunrise, where he dozed and let his horses graze until dusk.

One more night he jogged south along the old Whoop-up Trail that led to the Yellowstone and beyond into Wyoming. This was the trail the Flying U would expect him to take, but it seemed the most feasible for the time being, so he kept to it until he had crossed the Musselshell. Then, because of his stubbornness, he swung sharply off that road on to a trail that led westward, and after that, because the country was strange to him, he rode by daylight. Where, he neither knew nor cared, so long as he was lost to the Flying U.

CHAPTER NINE

THE CAMP IN THE CANYON

A gust of wind blowing up the canyon from the east brought with it a faint tang of sage smoke. By his own supper fire Chip caught the unmistakable odor and turned, startled as a skittish horse. The rabbit haunch he was broiling sagged and began to scorch before he lifted it up off the coals. His eyes and his mouth hardened a little, as he stared back down the way he had come.

Swift mental review of the trail he had followed told him that the fire must be close; just down around the next turn, in fact. That was where the canyon leveled off with good grass bottom and the creek running in easy shallows. He had been tempted to camp down there himself, but the same stubborn anger that had sent him off on strange trails drove him on a little farther before he would stop. He was glad now that it had, since he had no wish for neighbors. Horses you could bank on. But the less he saw of men the better he would be pleased. They were all traitors at heart—if ever he trusted any man again, he hoped someone would kindly brain him with an axe.

Nevertheless, as he impaled the meat more securely on its forked stick and held it again over the coals, that smoke smell nagged at his thoughts and drove his spirits deeper into the pit of gloom that had submerged them lately. He couldn't help speculating upon that campfire, wondering who was down there. No one he knew, of course—he had purposely headed into unknown country when he left the Flying U. But it was funny they had reached the Pass so soon after himself, for the trail ran straight out across a bald, level bench for miles until it wormed into this canyon split through the barrier mountains. There hadn't been so much as a distant cloud of dust rising like smoke behind him to show that travelers were on their way to the Pass.

It certainly was queer. And to make it seem more so, Mike walked out to the end of his picket rope and stood staring down that way, a wisp of grass clamped between his teeth while he looked and listened. Trail wise, that horse. Too wise to concern himself with strange horses or men unless they came close enough to force themselves upon his attention. Friends he could spot a mile off—and now he was registering eagerness. Suddenly he threw up his head to whinny loud greeting down the canyon.

Chip would have none of that. "You Mike! Cut that out!" Although his voice was low, it carried plenty of menace.

Mike started violently, glanced aside at his master and back down the canyon, gazing fixedly toward the wafted smoke. By every look and action he was trying to say that some horse or man he knew and liked was down around that turn.

Yet the three-year-colt, Silver, gave no sign of interest. Old Jeff didn't count. He wouldn't prick an ear if the whole Flying U cavvy came jingling up the canyon. Filling his belly now with grass was all he thought or cared about. But it was funny that Silver had nothing to say about that camp down below.

Chip's moody eyes brightened a little as they rested on the sleek chestnut sorrel, with the silvery mane and tail. From the day when he had lifted the gangling foal to its feet and dried it off with a grain sack, he had given that colt all the proud affection a quiet, self-contained young fellow could bestow. Showed him where his dinner was and held him steady on his legs while he learned to suck. Taught him tricks, talked to him like a human.

There wasn't a man on the Flying U range, or a horse either, that Silver didn't know and have a definite opinion of. Strangers he gave the go-by, unless they came fiddling around him, and then he'd mighty quick show them where they stood with him. And if there was anyone down at that camp he knew, he'd be on his way down there right now to say howdy. Yet Mike was eager, on his toes to go and see someone, and the colt never paid the slightest attention. It certainly was queer.

Chip poured himself a cup of coffee, raked fried potatoes and corn from the frying pan to his plate, broke a piece from the cold bannock he had saved from breakfast and settled himself to his supper, biting into the tender browned rabbit haunch with his strong white teeth. That rabbit was an extra delicacy added to his menu when it had hopped brazenly into camp after supper was started. He had held back his meal for it. But even as he ate, two deep creases stood between his dark eyebrows and his glance kept straying down the canyon.

Why didn't Silver show the same interest as Mike? If one of the Flying U boys were trailing him up—it would be just like Weary to try and coax him back—Silver would certainly be piking off down there, first sound or smell he got of him or his horse. If not someone from the Flying U, who else would make Mike act like that? Not that it mattered; not a damn bit.

Yet it did matter enough to occupy his thoughts while he ate and washed his dishes, packing everything neatly back into place in the box that held his cooking outfit. It mattered enough to send him down the canyon afterwards, walking slim and straight through the dusk, his big hat uncompromisingly tilted over his eyebrows.

He did not want to be seen but merely to see. When he reached the abrupt turn where the rock wall came out and shouldered the canyon sharply aside, he left the gravelly ruts of the road and took to the green grass carpeting the moist ground near the shallow creek. Some grim encounters of the past had bred caution in strange places. The six-shooter which hung snug at his side he moved forward a little, shifting the belt that sagged loosely with its weight of full cartridges.

He was not looking for trouble—never was, for that matter; but neither would he dodge it. Abruptly he caught the sound of horses cropping the grass near by. One sneezed and he caught a whiff of strong sweat odor. He moved silently away, behind a clump of bushes, setting his feet down carefully in the grass.

Had it been light enough to read brands, he would have gone closer, but there was nothing to be gained now by creating a disturbance among them. All he wanted was to identify the campers.

He walked on slowly for another fifty yards and stopped beside a young cottonwood to listen. The breeze kept rustling the leaves and smaller branches, but he thought he heard the mutter of a voice somewhere behind him. He turned and made his way stealthily in that direction, but the sound had ceased.

Puzzled and with a vague uneasiness growing in his mind, he veered away from the creek a few steps and halted again beside a bush, drawing in deep slow breaths through his nostrils, sorting the odors that came to him. Crushed grass blades, the delicate fragrance of wild roses, the tang of sage that pressed against his knee—and something else; the unmistakable smell of charred wood that has been lately wet. A doused fire, without a doubt.

Leaning out beyond the screening bush, he looked to left and right, and suddenly drew back out of sight. So close that the small sound startled him a match was struck. Through cautiously parted branches he peered out as the little flame flared up, outlining a bold profile etched against the blackness beyond. A strange face, thin and swarthy, straight black hair falling over the right temple and a high beak of a nose with a fresh scar down along the side from bridge to swollen nostril—

"Cut that out!" a low voice snarled. "What the hell's the matter with you? Cigarette smoke's a dead giveaway. Take a chaw, why don't yuh?"

The match flame died under a blown breath. "Aw, you got the willies. It's safe enough—"

Chip waited some minutes longer, heard no more than a wordless grunt, saw nothing whatever and retreated under cover of a rising whisper of wind, little wiser than before. It was no one from the Flying U— he was positive of that much. So it was none of his business who they were or why they had doused their fire.

"Darned chumps," he told himself scornfully, as he made his way cautiously up the canyon, "if they're so scared, they'd no business to turn their horses loose so close to the road." No business to camp there, either. A bunch of half-wits, in his opinion. Tenderfeet, most likely, afraid of Indians or outlaws.

Nevertheless, he could not feel exactly comfortable in his own camp. Without explaining to himself just why he did so, he shouldered his bedroll and picked his way into the edge of the nearest grove before he would spread his blankets and crawl in. Even then he could not sleep, though it was not altogether the thought of his neighbors that held him awake. Through the lace pattern of branches he stared up at the quiet stars, watching them brush thin veils of cloud from before their eyes so that they could look at the world below. But he was not thinking of the stars.

In the five days and nights since he had ridden out of Flying U coulee, his thoughts had been chained to the mental treadmill of his wrongs. Not until tonight could he forget just what it was Cal Emmett had said to precipitate that fight. Even J. G.'s unjust accusations were blurred in spots as his attention strayed from his grievances, swung again and again to that furtive camp down around the bend of the canyon.

He hoped he wasn't getting the jumps, just because somebody took a notion to douse his fire ahead of time. There wasn't any reason to suppose it concerned him in any way. If they were after him—and he could name several men who wouldn't mind taking a shot at him if they could get away with it—they wouldn't be sitting down there in the dark, afraid to smoke; they'd be nosing him out, trying to get a whack at him. And if they came prowling up here, Silver or Mike would let him know as quick as any watchdog.

All the same, he had a funny feeling about that camp down there. There was something scaley about that outfit; and that wasn't all—he wished he knew what ailed Mike. The darned chump kept wanting to go down there. He'd had to tie his head down to keep him from whinnying as though he was a mare that had lost her colt. Queer, how a horse always had to throw up his head before he could nicker—just a habit, maybe. Halter rope looped around a front leg wouldn't hurt anything—

With a muttered oath, he sat up in his blankets and reached for the makings. Maybe a smoke would help him get to sleep. He couldn't see what ailed him lately—he was getting fussy as any old woman. He rolled a cigarette, smoked it and found himself as wide awake as if it were noon. By the stars it was after midnight, and by the lightening of the canyon he knew the

73

moon was up. Clear as a bell—even those wisps of clouds gone—

Well, if he weren't going to sleep, he might as well be riding, by thunder. He'd get out of this blamed pass, into more open country, before he made camp. Ride until he was sleepy, anyway. It wouldn't hurt the horses—they must have their bellies full of grass by now, and he hadn't pushed them very hard. Hell, he was traveling to suit himself, wasn't he?

So he pulled on his clothes and carried his blankets out to where the rest of his pack had been left. His spirits lifted and he whistled under his breath while he saddled Mike and packed old Jeff, throwing the one-man diamond hitch with deft precision, even in that dim light. In less than fifteen minutes he was in the saddle, Jeff and the colt Silver swinging in behind him. Without a backward glance, he left the camp that had looked so desirable at sunset.

He rode in shadow, the late moon silvering the farther cliffs, making mystery of the trail he followed, thrilling him vaguely with half-promises of adventure, of new experiences waiting ahead. Without thinking of his reasons for it, he was glad he had decided to ride on, glad that he didn't know what lay ahead on the trail. It was all mystery up the canyon—

Abruptly the mystery flowed in behind him, seemed to reach out and claw for a hold on him. For, faintly carried on the breeze that still crept up the canyon, there came the distant *"Pow-w!—pow-w!—pow-pow-w!"* and, finally, another savage bark as someone emptied a six-shooter, back down there at that camp where one

74

man thought it wasn't safe to let cigarette smoke drift out into the dark.

Instinctively Chip's hand tightened the reins, pulling Mike half around in the trail. His scalp tingled a little at the nape of his neck. It was not the first time he had heard canyon walls fling back the sound of shooting in the night, and he could picture the spurts of orange light that marked the shots. He knew too the thin whine of a bullet zipping past—knew exactly how it felt to have one plough into flesh and bone. It was not because he was unseasoned that he felt his skin crawl at the sound.

Just at first he could not explain the creepy feeling he had. He was half tempted to go back and see what all the ruckus was about, though gun-fighting was not the kind of adventure he wanted; not a game he cared to buy into unless he knew what he was doing it for. Let 'em fight it out. It wasn't any concern of his.

And yet, as he sat there on his horse listening and staring down into the patchy light and darkness of the canyon, it seemed to him as if somehow it did concern him. Improbable conjectures flashed through his mind. Someone he knew—no friend—some enemy perhaps. One of Big Butch's gang—but that was impossible. How would they know he was traveling this way? Or if they did, why had they stayed down there in that darkened camp while their horses fed and rested? Why hadn't they come on up and tackled him?

No, it wasn't that. Mike wouldn't get all excited over any of those jaspers, and he never did throw in with any of their horses; wouldn't stir out of his tracks for them.

He rode on when the silence gave forth no other sound and told himself it was no concern of his. It couldn't be. And yet some warning instinct told him that it was.

CHAPTER TEN
HORSES DON'T LIE

As the road crawled persistently upward, the canyon walls drew in, heaps of rock rubble spilled down their precipitous slopes. No more level bottoms, which in this season became tiny meadows; even the creek had dodged into a brushy gulch as the canyon narrowed to a steep rocky gorge, the road still clinging to its southern wall. How far it was to the summit of the pass Chip did not know, but he saw that there was no stopping now until he reached some valley on the other side.

The three horses plodded steadily upward, sweating even in that cool breeze that still blew up the canyon. His hand brushed down along Mike's shoulder came away wet, and Chip called himself a fool for pulling out of a good camp in the middle of the night. He should have stayed and given the horses a good night's rest.

It wasn't the sweat that worried Mike, however. He still insisted that there was something behind him he would like to investigate. Whenever the trail swung north to edge around some bold outthrust of rock, he would turn his head and gaze back down the pass, trying to catch a glimpse of something or someone his nose told him was coming along behind.

Twice he whinnied loudly, swinging crosswise in the trail—but all he got for answer was a taste of the rein ends across his rump. His efforts to tell what he knew put Chip on the alert, however. When the swing of the trail brought the lower reaches into view, he would turn and ride with one hand on the cantle, his body twisted sidewise while he watched. But even with the moon riding high, the light was uncertain on the road, shaded as it was by the canyon wall while the northern slopes and bold crags and cliffs stood in silver light.

He could see nothing. Half the time the road behind him was blacked out completely and the slow wind pushing up the pass whooed and whistled among the rocks, brushing the smooth surfaces with a whisper as of silken skirts. His shoulders lifted in dismissal, trying to shrug away the mystery. Immediately he grinned to himself, thinking that he might as well have stayed in camp, so far as his mood was concerned. He hadn't found mental ease on the trail, that was sure. He hadn't gained a darned thing, in fact, except a guilty conscience for the way he was imposing on his horses, making them take the trail at midnight.

An hour before daybreak he crossed the bleak windy summit, the horses striking sparks with their calked shoes on the smooth rock. Stirrups thrust forward, body slanted backward against the steep descent, he balanced his weight for Mike, as he rode down toward black forest. At dawn he was riding through cathedral aisles of whispery pines, rose-tinted clouds tangled in their tops. The horses trod softly on the thick carpet of brown pine needles, with only the faint squeak of saddle leather, the clink of spur chains to mark their passing. Patches of old snow lay banked in the shade where the sun never came.

A little later, Chip killed a grouse with the swift sure aim of a sharp rock picked off a boulder as he passed and flung with quick boyish zest. Just why he did not shoot instead he made no attempt to explain, even to himself. Without dismounting, he leaned from the saddle and picked up the bird, tying it to his saddle fork by the neck as he rode along.

Now he would camp as soon as he found grass, and he turned aside down the parklike slope, following a snow-fed stream and looking back now and then, secretly pleased to see how soon the road was lost to sight behind him, and how slight the marks his three horses left among needles and dry cones.

The sun was just beginning to gild the peaks seen raggedly through the pine tops. As Mike picked his careful way down the carpeted slope, following the general direction of the tumbling creek, far off and faint somewhere ahead there came the sweet, rippling notes of a meadowlark's song. To Chip that brief melody was more than a song; it was a promise. He reined Mike more to the right and rode forward with an eager expectancy.

Presently he emerged from the forest into a natural meadow like a green saucer, rimmed with the darker green of the forest. An ancient lake bed, probably, made fertile through uncounted seasons. Straight across, perhaps five hundred yards away, he glimpsed a group of balsam firs standing clannishly out from the pines, their thick dark branches drooping to the ground like the graceful swirl of a dancer's ruffled skirt. With a deep sigh of satisfaction, he left the brawling creek to wander where it would, and rode straight out and across.

"Now, Mike, maybe you'll settle down and behave yourself," he remarked, as he swung down beside the balsam clump and began to unsaddle. "You've been seeing spooks all night, and you want to cut it out, now." With a mile or so of forest and then the meadow to cut them off from the road, it seemed likely that Mike would forget his notions.

And yet his distinct feeling of relief shamed him a bit. With a little less experience, he might have mistaken it for fear and gone brazenly back to prove himself. But he knew he had not been afraid, back there in the pass. He didn't quite know what it was that had ailed him; a hunch, maybe. A feeling there was something he'd better sidestep while he had the chance. Whatever it was, he had left it behind him. It didn't do to let yourself get funny ideas. Better deal with facts and let it go at that.

Best camping spot here, he presently told himself, he'd ever run across. A few rods beyond the balsams was a little spring creek, and the place was sheltered. He could cut balsam boughs for his bed and not have to carry them a mile, and he'd bet, by thunder, tonight he would sleep! He'd get this grouch out of his system before he rode another mile. He'd been like a she bear with a sore head ever since he quit the Flying U.

So he unpacked Jeff between the tiny stream and the balsam thicket, cut boughs and wove them into a springy mattress waist deep, spread his blankets on top, built a fire and cooked his grouse and for a time forgot his troubles and his perplexities in sheer physical content.

Tired though he was, he would not yield to the temptation of that high bed yet, but continued whacking off dead twigs and the branches tangled beneath the canopy of higher boughs, hewing himself two sizable spaces beneath the close-growing trees. Those thatched boughs above would turn water like a shingled roof, he thought. Turn the biting winds too, when he had laced in a few thick branches around the sides.

Gosh, why not stay here all summer? He could drop down into Big Timber and bring back a packload of grub. One trip, and he'd have enough for three months. He'd live like an Indian, by thunder! Hunt and fish and do as he darn pleased; draw pictures without having a dozen fellows hanging over his shoulders, gawping and passing bright remarks. About the time fall roundup started, he could ride on down into cattle country and get himself a job; but now—he'd be free as the wind.

Ever since he could remember he had dreamed of living all by himself in some remote, high mountain valley such as this, and here was his dream come true, real for as long as he wanted it so. His step grew buoyant as he planned, his eyes lost their brooding bitterness. The snick-snick of the axe cleaning the tree trunks of their frowsy dead twigs, the tangy fragrance of the balsam carried a healing balm to his very soul.

He never knew that he began to whistle over the work, never realized that the whistling turned into a song, whose mournful words never reached his consciousness at all, but whose plaintive melody made pleasing accompaniment to his vagrant thoughts:

"There's a sob in ev–'ry bree–eze
And a — sigh comes from — the tree–ees,
A–and the meadow — lark now sings — a sad–der
     la–ay —
   To–da–dah — ta–dah — ta dah dah,
   Tada dah — ta–dah — ta–dah–h —
Where the sil–v'ry Col — o–rado winds its wa–ay."

Just beyond the balsams Mike, on his picket rope, blew pollen and dew from his nostrils with a bubbling sound. His straight black tail switched with a mechanical rhythm, warning flies from his rumps still rough with dried sweat from the long wearisome climb. Old Jeff grazed loose near by, sides wet from having rolled in the dewy grass. Farther out, almost at the opposite rim of the little basin, Silver grazed venturesomely by himself, picking and choosing amongst lavish abundance, a dancey spring in every unstudied motion.

As Chip paused in his work to look for the colt, Silver moved slowly out into the first slanting rays of sunlight that had found their way into the meadow. His glossy coat shone with glints of bronze sharply contrasted with the argent gleam of mane and tail tossing in the wind. Calm proprietorship was revealed in every move he made. It was his meadow, every inch of it his own.

With an understanding grin, Chip returned to his task. Already his ideas had expanded. When he finally cleared away the litter, carrying it across the little open space and piling it out of sight in the brush, he had a roomy bedroom and a separate kitchen enclosed in living balsam boughs. He had a hole dug in the shallow creek bed where he could fill his bucket with one swoosh and a dip, and he had enough rocks carried into camp for a fireplace.

He was sitting back on his heels sucking a skinned knuckle and damning the rock that had slipped, when Mike suddenly stopped nipping grass and stood staring fixedly at a point out beyond the thicket, a wisp of grass clamped in his teeth. He looked exactly as he had done last evening, except that now he did not seem eager and he showed no desire to whinny a greeting.

A premonitory thrill of resentment broke the spell of Chip's blithe mood. He frowned and the old bitterness was in his face as he walked out where he could see. A man had ridden into the basin from the south and was headed straight for Silver, feeding unconscious of any danger over against the line of the forest.

Chip's mouth drew in against his teeth. He stepped back, picked up his rifle and moved out again into full view. It was evident that the rider had not noticed any sign of a camp—indeed, the balsams hid it well. He was riding slowly, as if he did not want to startle the colt, and even as Chip covered him with the rifle, he took down his rope and shook out the loop.

"Hey!" Chip called sharply. "What do you think you're after?"

The rider's head jerked around. His hand swept back to his holstered gun, halted and flung up empty when he saw the rifle looking his way. The rope dangled in loose coils across the saddle in front of him as the other hand went up.

"Goin' after my horse," he shouted grudgingly. "Anything wrong about that?"

"I'd tell a man there is! There certainly is no horse of yours in this meadow. You better drift."

Taken aback, the horseman hesitated, eyeing Chip, who made no move. "Your ante," he called sullenly. "Any objection if I put my hands down?"

"Be damned sure they're in front of you, then."

The stranger lowered his arms with care, reined his horse toward the balsam thicket and came on slowly, hands clasped upon the saddle horn. A hard-featured range man, lean and long, with little to distinguish him from a hundred others; one of a type long familiar to the range. When he had covered half the distance, he spoke again, his voice mildly complaining, edged with suspicion.

"My horse strayed off from camp, down the road a piece. If that ain't him over there, my eyesight shore is failin'!"

"Better buy yourself a pair of specs, then. That happens to be my horse over there."

The stranger half turned in the saddle and took another long look. When his eyes came back to study Chip's face, they suddenly squinted with surprise. The rifle had somehow disappeared and a silver-mounted forty-five was staring at him instead. He shrugged in sour acceptance of the situation.

"Well, I make it a rule never to call a man a liar when he's got a gun on me," he drawled, "but I still say that looks a hell of a lot like my flax-maned geldin', over there. He ain't a horse you'd easy mistake. I'd 'a' bet there wasn't another like him in the country."

Chip's mouth twitched. "Well, it's easy enough to prove who he belongs to. Stay right where you are, stranger—and watch."

From the corner of his eye he darted a glance toward the colt, looked back at the horseman. Unexpectedly he shouted, "You, Silver! *Come and get it!*"

With a kick and a flourish of tossing head and lifted rump, the three-year-old wheeled and came racing across the meadow, ducked sharply away from the strange horseman, snorted and stared, then trotted springy-kneed to where Chip stood. Outthrust lip pointed and quivering with desire, he reached out, smelling for the sugar he had been taught to expect.

"Still think he's your horse?" Chip offered a white cube with his left hand to the colt.

The stranger shook his head. "No-o, I reckon that settles the argument, all right. Looks like he's your horse."

"You bet your sweet life he's mine." In spite of himself, a boyish note of pride crept into Chip's voice.

"Horses don't lie—but just the same, he's enough like my Flax to be his twin. A little younger, maybe— not much, though." His eyes turned thoughtfully to Chip's face. "What'll yuh take for him, young feller?"

CHAPTER ELEVEN
CHIP MAKES A TRADE

A pulse began to hammer in Chip's throat. Lips tightly closed, he drew breath sharply through his nostrils. Little, furtive hopes went racing through his mind, trying to escape the throttling clutch of stern logic. Another horse exactly like Silver? One a year older, maybe? It couldn't be the one he hoped it was— and yet, maybe it was—but such luck never happened—not to him, anyway. But if it were—

He was shaking his head. "There isn't money enough in Montana to buy this horse," he was saying brusquely. "Raised him from a foal." And he added more casually, while the colt thrust his soft quivering nose over Chip's shoulder, breathing on his neck, "Kind of a pet."

"Yeah, I see he is." The man's sidelong glance took in Jeff and Mike. "You're pretty well hooked up with horses. Want to sell that brown?" And he answered Chip's sharp questioning glance, "Buyin' horses is my business. Never pass up a trade."

That hammering pulse in Chip's throat almost choked him. He had to swallow before he could speak and be sure of his voice.

"If you buy and trade, chances are you sell," he observed tentatively.

"Sure, I sell. You in the market?" A keen, predatory look sharpened all his features. His gaze narrowed on Chip.

"Well, that depends. That horse you say is like Silver, here—if he's a perfect match, I might buy him. If the price is right." What it cost him to speak so carelessly no one would ever know.

"Say, he's a dead ringer for that colt! Taller and heavier, is all. Give this one time to fill out some and I bet you couldn't tell 'em apart." He paused, then added craftily, while he rolled a cigarette, "I could make a good price on that geldin' too. He's a valuable horse; got good bottom and can run like a streak—"

"Where'd you pick him up?" To save his life, Chip could not hold his voice to an easy indifference. The last words broke a little. He hoped the man wouldn't notice.

"Hunh?" The trader was busy lighting his cigarette and seemed unconscious of any emotion in Chip's face or tone. "Well, I traded a feller a couple of old plugs for 'im. He was goin' on into the mountains on a prospectin' trip, and he wanted something steadier. Flax—I call him that—he's a fancy horse. Like that one there. Make a dandy saddle horse for some city swell; lots of style, right up on the bit and full of springs— dead ringer for that colt," he repeated. "That's what I figured on doin' with him. Wait till I swing back around toward Butte or Helena, maybe, and sell him to some rich guy. I could get a fancy price for him."

He exhaled a thin blue cloud, watching Chip with sly, sidelong glances. "Trouble is, I've got a bunch of horses to deliver to a cow outfit down the other side of Bozeman. Flax, he's too full of life for them old cow ponies. Keeps me chasin' him up all the while. Like this morning." He estimated Mike with quick, measuring looks. "I oughta be on my way, right now, instead of huntin' that flax-maned road-runner all over the map."

He had covered his appraisal with too much talk. Chip had time to pull himself together. He slid his gun into its holster and fed Silver more sugar. His interest seemed to have gone lukewarm. He could match wits now, he thought, with any slick trader.

"Well, I certainly couldn't pay any fancy price," he said, "even if the horse suited me. I've got about all the livestock I can feed. I just had a notion that if I could match this colt, I'd break 'em to harness and have me a dandy buggy team. No particular use for one. Be just a luxury and I don't know as I could afford it, anyway."

The stranger threw away his cigarette. His whole manner subtly changed. He became all at once briskly amiable.

"Suit yourself, uh course. I'll just round the son of a gun up and lead him over for you to see. As I said, I'd be willin' to knock off some, just to get him off my hands and save swingin' around through Butte. Like to have you take a look at him, anyway. You don't have to buy, if you don't want to."

"Damned right, I don't," drawled Chip. "I'll look him over, though." He achieved an air almost of condescension, which implied that he would be doing the horse-buyer a favor if he bothered to examine the animal.

"Well, I'll scout around some more of these little meadows and see if I run acrost him. See yuh later."

With a perfunctory gesture of farewell, Chip's arm dropped over Silver's neck, long fingers combing out the tangles in the crinkly mane as if nothing else concerned him. Until the horseman rode out of sight among the bushes he kept up the play. Then suddenly he laid his cheek against the satiny jaw of the colt and drew a long sigh of released tension.

"What'd you say if we got your big brother back?" he asked softly, one hand going up to stroke the colt's brown muzzle. "You remember Rummy—hunh? Remember how he used to tease and devil you when you were just a pot-bellied suckin' colt that didn't think of anything but getting your dinner? I guess you don't. Two years is a long time for a youngster like you to remember. Bet you've forgotten your mother, even. Sylvia—Lord, it'd be too much luck for one man if he was to lead Sylvia over here too!"

He patted and smoothed, slipping a piece of comb out of a hip pocket and combing the heavy forelock banged just above the colt's eyelids. And while he combed and fussed, he talked on in the low murmur a man finds only for his horse or his sweetheart—but mostly for his horse.

"If that's Rummy he was talking about—it's got to be. Couldn't be another horse in the country just like you. Hunh? Kinda stuck on yourself, ain't yuh? Well, when Rummy gets here, I just bet he'll take you down a notch or two! He'll be the boss, or he'll sure know why not! Only difference between you is in disposition, and that don't show much on the surface—How'll you like to be bullied again, hunh? The way you used to tag him around—just asking for trouble. Then I'd have to buy into the scrap and pull him off yuh. I expect," he chuckled happily. "it'll be the same old story—keep me busy protecting you!"

He fell silent, thinking. Silver stood with head bowed, eyes closed, lost in the ecstasy of his master's caressing touch. Chip's eyes shone beneath their heavy lashes. The mask of cool indifference had dropped from his face and his mouth was tender and sorrowful and stern, smiling when his mood changed with the pictures conjured by his thoughts.

"Damn Big Butch! Him and his gang—if they hadn't tried to steal the Flying U blind, I wouldn't have had to sell Rummy and Sylvia." His eyes stormed at the tragedy of that parting, then softened again. "Wouldn't let *you* go, though—'cause you weren't worth a cent! Know that? Ab-so-lute-ly worthless! Didn't have the nerve to ask two-bits for yuh! Be ashamed to offer yuh as a gift! Just a worthless cuss nobody'd have on a bet!" His whole face glowed as it never had for a girl. "No good! Just an ornery, dawgoned runt that ain't worth his salt—or his sugar, either!"

That last-mentioned dainty struck a responsive thought in Silver. He snuffed and rooted and bared his teeth in a threat of what he would do if he didn't get a lump right then. And for that he had both ears grabbed and twisted in mock savagery.

"Bite me, would yuh? How about me chewing an ear off? Like that!" White teeth of the boy nipped gently the ear tip handiest. In retaliation, the colt tilted his head downward and pinched Chip's leg with a bite more severe than he intended.

"Ouch! Cut that out, dawgone yuh! I'll sell yuh to that trader for a dollar and a half! I'll trade yuh for Rummy, that's what. If I've got to be chawed and kicked and tromped on, by gosh, I'll let a *real* horse do it! Take your damn sugar and shut up about it. And you come on around here where I can keep an eye on yuh. That feller may be all right, and he may have thought you were Rummy—if it is Rummy—but just the same, he won't have another chance to make the same mistake. You go on a picket rope, you ornery, knock-kneed, hammer-headed, wall-eyed old skate, before somebody leads yuh off and shoots yuh just to put you outa your misery!" And he added to himself, as he led the colt around behind the trees, where he got a coil of rope and a picket pin:

"Things may be just what they're cracked up to be. But when in Rome, keep your eyes peeled for the Romans!"

The colt tethered safely within ten rods of camp, he proceeded to take another precaution quite as important. He retired to his improvised bedroom, pulled up his shirt and unbuckled his money belt. Several months' wages in gold and currency made a modest padding for the pockets. Twice he counted, chewing a corner of his lip over the financial problem he faced.

He really needed every cent of it. Being broke among strangers didn't appeal to him in the least. It was crazy to think of buying another horse.

Doubt seized him. "Chances are he was just making a damn fool of me. Thought he'd rope him a good horse when he thought nobody was around to catch him at it." He scowled at the unpleasant possibility. "Just a common ordinary horse thief, most likely. Had to think up a slick excuse when I jumped him. Hell, *he* don't own any flax-maned chestnut gelding—"

A thought stopped him, started that hammer going again inside him. Funny that fellow should describe a horse exactly like Rummy must be now; a year or so older than Silver, bigger and heavier—how had he come to say that? "Anyway, Benson wouldn't sell Rummy. He was too damn anxious to get him. Still—"

He counted out a hundred dollars, put the rest back in the belt, and pulled it around his slim muscular body next his bare skin. The fellow had just been stringing him, probably. Still, it wouldn't hurt anything to be ready. You never knew—

A shrill whinny brought him outside in two long strides. "Mike! What the devil ails you? Quit it, you damn fool!"

His voice shook. He had trouble with his breathing, as if he had just run at top speed across the meadow. For Mike was dancing and circling at the end of his rope, shaking his head, then throwing it up to stare with an almost tragic eagerness. Again that clarion call of his shattered the divine serenity of the forest-walled basin.

Chip had to force himself to walk out from behind the trees and see for himself. It wouldn't do to yell and throw up his hat, he told himself fiercely, believing the tidings Mike was giving him in every way he knew. A fellow had to hold himself together. He couldn't let the tears roll down his cheeks—Lord, he was a bigger fool than that damned crazy cayuse.

So he threatened Mike with the toe of his boot and walked out with his hands on his hips, fighting down the excitement that made his knees wobbly. For there in the meadow, looking in no hurry whatever, came the horse buyer, leading a high-stepping chestnut horse with crinkly mane and tail as silvery as the colt on the picket rope could boast. Leading the one horse Chip had ever loved as worshipfully as he did Silver; the three-year-old's full brother, sacrificed once on the altar of his loyalty to J. G. and the Flying U; leading a miracle, so far as Chip was concerned.

But none of this showed in his manner, as he sauntered forward. "Sure didn't take you long," he remarked with a drawl.

The man came to a stand, and Rummy condescended a nicker to Mike by way of greeting, then whirled and lifted his shining rump. Chip bit his tongue painfully, shutting off the old familiar yell that had rung in the gelding's ears uncounted times in the past. A yell he would have recognized and obeyed with a shake of his beautiful head, Chip hadn't a doubt.

"Found him right over in the next meadow. Dead ringer for yourn, like I said."

Chip looked Rummy over with veiled eyes. "Well,

no reason why he wouldn't be, I guess. That horse happens to be one I sold two years ago. Full brother of this other one. You got him over near Billings, didn't you?"

The man's eyes flickered. "Me, I never been to Billings. No, I traded for him, like I told yuh. Feller wanted to go prospecting. He sure is a dandy—"

"He's a devil," Chip corrected coldly, hungry eyes permitting themselves no more than a quick slighting glance. "You can't tell me anything about that son of a gun. I know him from a colt. If there's no devilment around, he'll stir up some."

The trader shifted uneasily in the saddle. "Why, pshaw! There ain't a mean bone in that horse's body! You got him all wrong. Full of play now and then— he's got good life. But if he ever was mean, he sure has outgrown it. Gentle as a kitten now."

"Yes?" Chip managed to sound extremely doubtful. He reached for the makings and began to roll a smoke, walking toward Rummy to hide how his fingers were trembling. "Well, what'll you take for him, devil and all?"

CHAPTER TWELVE
THERE'S ONLY ONE RUMMY

Until the horse buyer was well out in the meadow, Chip stood where he was and watched. His underlip smarted where the skin was bitten through. The salty taste of blood from the tiny cut was in his mouth. There went Mike, trotting reluctantly behind his new owner, lead rope tight as the brown horse pulled back against it.

"Judas!" whispered Chip between closed teeth, and swallowed at the dry lump in his throat. "I oughta be shot for that." Troubled eyes turned to Rummy. "You'll certainly have to go some to take old Mike's place. You'll have to deliver the goods. For two cents—"

Rummy turned from staring after them and looked at Chip. For the first time, that voice seemed to hold for him a special significance. With a smooth rippling of glossy bronze coat and a toss of his head, he moved closer, thrusting out his lip as soft as the skin of a mole. Big, lustrous eyes begged.

"Kinda remember me, hunh?" Mechanically Chip's hand went into his pocket, came out with a piece of cut-loaf sugar. "Kinda remember that too, don't yuh?"

Suddenly his arms went around the firm, arched neck. For just a minute his face was buried in the thick mane. When he lifted it, a new content shone in his eyes, a hurt had been pushed far back where no one would see. He glanced out across the basin and saw it empty of everything except the busy meadowlarks. He smoothed and patted, stood back to admire the perfect animal into which Rummy had grown. With a forced smile, he offered another lump.

"I sure thought a heap of Mike," he said slowly, "but—hell, there's only one Rummy. I'd tell a man. That right, old socks? Come on around here and say howdy to your baby brother. Bet yuh won't know him, either."

Rummy didn't. The two horses met with slow deliberate steps, gravely touched noses, then suddenly exploded into squeals and bared teeth, Rummy trying to take a chunk out of Silver's neck, Silver standing his ground and fighting back, ears flattened against his head. With a delighted oath, Chip sprang for his rope, shook out the loop and noosed Rummy, cuffing him with his hat and promising death in various unpleasant forms.

"And when I get yuh in a pasture somewhere where you both have got an even break," he finished grimly, "I'll let Silver and you fight it out. And I hope he licks the livin' tar outa you. Pickin' on a horse when he's staked out and can't handle himself! Ain't you ashamed of yourself?"

Rummy shook an impenitent head, pushed out his lip and brazenly asked for more sugar. He got it and heard himself called a bad name for good measure. Then Silver made it plain that no such partiality would be tolerated in that camp and won his point and a four-square lump.

So presently the two beautiful animals, alike in everything but size—which time would equalize—were standing contentedly side by side, licking their master's two palms for the last sweet grains. And with his hat knocked backward and askew on his brown head, Chip was laughing with the old boyish chuckle in his voice, all the bitterness wiped from his thin good-looking face. With his new balsam camp and his two flax-maned horses in this remote Eden of the mountains, kings had nothing he wanted instead. He was rich. He hadn't a care in the world or a wish ungranted. (Which was exactly the mood he needed to balance the state of mind he had been in for the past week.)

While the sun shone into the basin, that mood held. Just for the excuse he wanted for prolonging his joy of possession, he got out currycomb and brush and groomed Rummy as long as he could find a hair unsmoothed. Afterward he saddled and galloped him around the meadow; roped off him, shot off him, sent him forward in a dead run and reined him this way and that, pretending he was cutting a critter out of a herd. He rode full tilt to an imaginary deadline and "spiked his tail", stopping in two stiff-legged jumps.

The result rather amazed him, well as he knew that strain of breeding; a strain which the rancher Benson, over near Billings, had recognized at sight. A peach of a horse, even if he hadn't been home folks. A hundred dollars and Mike to boot had seemed pretty stiff, but it wasn't. Mike was a dandy saddle horse, but he couldn't hold a candle to Rummy, any way you looked at him. Rummy was younger, faster, quick as greased lightning. That deep chest of his proved he was a stayer, and he had the intelligence to go with it. Not that he was slamming Mike any; he was just outclassed, that was all. Between the two, he had made the only choice possible.

He rode back to the balsam thicket and unsaddled, staking Rummy out with Mike's rope and picket pin where he could fraternize with Silver and yet couldn't reach him for any devilment. He finished the fireplace, cooked his dinner and ate with his eyes turned to watch his new-found pet. With a sigh of complete relaxation, he lay down for a nap, his face dropped on his folded arms where he had only to lift one eyebrow and open that eye to see Silver and Rummy—particularly Rummy. And before he knew it, he was sound asleep, healing forces from his happiness pouring through his six feet of weary body.

When he awoke, the sun was poised above the tree-tops beyond the meadow and a chill had crept into the air. He sat up with a start, looking first to make sure his horses were all right. Their quiet feeding reassured him, but his inner elation had somehow left him while he slept. Sitting on the ground with his back against a tree and his knees drawn up, he rolled a cigarette and stared absently at Rummy while he smoked.

Trifles disregarded while his blood went leaping at his luck swarmed now like midges before his mental vision. Mike, last night—that was Rummy down the canyon he heard or smelled, or both! Funny he should forget all about that until now. Sure, it was Rummy. Look how Mike performed when that horse trader led Rummy into camp. Mike knew that colt he'd thought the world of when they were together; two years isn't so long for a horse to remember—

While he let out a mouthful of smoke through half-closed lips, remorse had him by the throat again. Poor old Mike. It was a damn shame to separate them again. Didn't mean a thing to Rummy, but it sure meant a whole heap to Mike.

Then another thought darted into his mind. That shooting down the canyon. That needed explaining, by thunder! This fellow could tell a lot about that if he wanted to, and Chip bet the trader would a heap rather it wasn't told. Pretty darned mysterious, when you came to think of it—and he'd pulled out right away with his horses; he must have got under way *pronto,* the way Mike had acted up all through the pass. Damn funny, that whole thing.

Well, that would put the fellow up here a little after Chip, and so—hell, he must have lost Rummy quick! A cold suspicion fastened itself in Chip's mind. Maybe he hadn't lost Rummy at all; maybe he just happened to see Silver over across the meadow and thought he'd get himself a mate for Rummy. He certainly had found Rummy darned soon; in about the time it would take him to ride back to a camp and rope the colt out of the bunch.

That possibility suggested others even more sinister. What if Rummy had been stolen? He took out the bill of sale and read it over. No, that looked all straight enough. A. B. Mosely was the fellow's name. A horse thief wouldn't give papers to be used against him or sign his name with all those flourishes. At least, Chip didn't believe he would be so simple.

But if this Mosely had mixed himself up in a shooting scrape last night and wanted to slip through the country as inconspicuously as possible, he certainly would jump at the first chance he had to get rid of a horse like Rummy. Anybody who saw his outfit would spot Rummy in a minute and remember him too. And that naturally argued against his having been stolen from Benson. No one but a fool would steal a horse like that and A. B. Mosely didn't look like a fool.

No, maybe everything was all straight and he really had mistaken Silver for Rummy. He could have, easily enough. In fact, if Rummy were loose and out of sight, he'd be almost sure to. No use getting suspicious, even if he didn't like A. B. Mosely's looks. He'd cross his bridges when he came to them. Right now he had nothing to worry about and a heap for which to be thankful.

He tossed the cigarette stub into his new fireplace and watered the horses, leading them one at a time to the little stream and taking twice as long with Rummy as he did with Silver, knowing all the while that he was acting like a kid with a full stocking on Christmas, and telling himself it was his own business and he was free to act as he pleased, thank the Lord. Furthermore, he wanted to take a good look at Rummy's brands, just to satisfy himself there had been no funny business going on.

But even though the brands looked all right and he could not lay a mental finger on any specific reason for doubt, he staked Rummy out in a new place so close to camp that he had to shorten the picket rope a little to keep him from nosing around the fireplace. Silver he tethered a few rods to the left of the trees, just beyond the spring. No definite reason for that, except he was still indulging himself in the childish impulse to take his most precious things to bed with him—or come as close to doing so as was practicable with two active young horses.

Old Jeff came up from the meadow to drink, stood

looking at Rummy with a mildly bewildered interest, turned and gave Silver a long ruminative stare, switched his tail and went back to his grazing. Chip laughed and thought he'd like to read Jeff's mind right then. He would bet that in horse language Jeff was saying, "Oh, hell, what's the use?"

He was still grinning over the small incident when he fell asleep on his aromatic bed of balsam boughs. No thought of his trouble with the Flying U came to harass him, even in his dreams. He was at peace with the world; or as nearly so as a wilful young fellow may expect to be even for a little while.

What woke him he could not tell, but suddenly his eyes were wide open and he was looking out under the branches of his tentlike tree, his vision cut off by the dark wall of forest across the creek. Breath held within his lungs, he listened for some disturbing sound and heard only the whisper of a breeze in the branches over his head; that and a wood rat's abrupt scamper near by.

Then Silver snorted—a loud sound which Chip understood as well as words. It said that something he did not like was altogether too close. Rummy took it up, and the trampling of the two horses brought him out of his blankets and feeling in the dark for his boots. While he was stamping the second one on his foot, he heard the thud of Rummy's heels landing on something solid. There was a grunt and the squeal of a horse.

"Jeff! Is that you making that ruction?" With his six-shooter in his hand, he ran out into the open. "What's the matter with you, anyway?"

Then, as a horse moved off, he heard a crackling of brush just out beyond Rummy, across the tiny creek, and sent a shot in that direction for luck. A bear, maybe, for the sound continued, growing fainter as he listened. He hadn't thought of that risk before. But away up here among the mountains—why, of course there would be mountain lion and bear—grizzlies, probably. If a bear had clawed Rummy—!

Jerking a lantern off the limb where he had hung it for emergencies, he lighted it in a hurry and went to make sure. Just beyond the fireplace the horse stood breathing gustily through flared nostrils. His head was up and he was staring, not at the bushes whence the noise of hurried departure had come, but out toward the meadow, beyond the balsam firs.

And that, Chip thought, was mighty queer. It couldn't be Jeff, and yet in the night, if he had come prowling into camp and these two were asleep, he might have startled them. And if he got too close to Rummy he'd get kicked, and serve him right. It might have been a deer come down to drink. The horses didn't act as if it were a bear—

He stood and listened, and he heard the beat of hoofs going away from camp. "Jeff, the old fool," he muttered. And then he gave a start and a gasp of astonishment. Out in the meadow, but more to the right of the thicket, Jeff blew his nostrils free of dew. No mistaking that snuffling sneeze.

Chip's eyebrows drew together. Even the mild-mannered Jeff would not be grazing so soon after getting a crack in the ribs from Rummy's heels. That sneeze sounded very much as if the old pack horse had not interrupted his contented feeding to go nosing around camp. So, then, what about that other horse? He was sure he had heard it—the soft, steady beat of a horse trotting over grass-carpeted sod.

"I must be getting the willies," Chip thought disgustedly. But he did not go back to his springy bed. He carried his blankets out into the open and slept—or tried to sleep—where every night sound came to his ears and he had only to lift his eyelids to see Rummy and Silver feeding close at hand.

CHAPTER THIRTEEN
THE TRAIL GOES ON

But the night was spoiled for sleeping except in short cat naps that brought little rest. For one thing, he had let the wild beauty of this spot betray him into camping too close to the deep woods beyond the tiny stream. All the beasts of the forest seemed to be abroad that night, hungry and hunting a meal. Squeaks and rustlings and the occasional cracking of brush kept him awake and made the horses fidgety; he could hear them walking uneasily within the radius of their picket ropes, listening prick-eared to every strange noise. As the night advanced, even old Jeff moved in for companionship and stood backed against the trees, his wise old eyes fixed upon the impenetrable shadows across the creek.

Well, they'd have to get used to it, that was all. When they got thoroughly located, he could turn them loose, maybe. No reason why he couldn't throw a fence around the meadow. Plenty of poles and it wouldn't take long to cut enough. A stake-and-rider fence would be the ticket—or anyway, a corral out there beyond the trees. They wouldn't be right on top of all the noise then. Bears wouldn't be apt to bother them in a corral—

He dozed and in his dreams went on planning. Trap. That's what he'd do. Ought to be dandy fur country, up here in the winter—And he dreamed that he was building himself a snug winter camp, with hay stacked beside a log stable and a winter's supply of grub stowed away in a warm cabin right beside the balsams. He had his trap line and was taking fur—

He awoke to the blare of a horse neighing some-where, and had a panicky moment, when he thought it was Rummy being driven off and trying to let his master know. Then, while he was pulling his wits together, Silver trumpeted a loud welcoming whinny, and Chip knew what had happened.

"Mike, by all that's holy!" he grunted, and felt for his rope as he threw off the blankets. Running into the open, he was in time to see the brown horse come thundering into camp, head and tail held high, nickering his joy at every step. Chip's face was a study as he tied the rope around Mike's neck and gave him an affectionate slap on the shoulder. "Now you've done it!" he growled. "What in thunder 'd you come back *here* for?"

He knew well enough—though he couldn't know just what Mike's coming portended. He did feel mighty uncomfortable watching the horses express their satisfaction over the reunion, and he had to remind himself again and again that Mike wasn't his horse any more, to pet and bully and feed sugar to and take care of, along with the rest. In A. B. Mosely's pocket was a bill of sale for Mike, and the sooner he came and got his horse, the better for all concerned.

But Mosely did not come. When the sun stood high and still there was no sight or sound of him, Chip saddled Rummy, took Mike on the lead rope and started off, Silver and Jeff trailing along behind as a matter of course. A faint trail of bent and trampled brush led him toward the trader's camp and he followed it impatiently, wanting the thing over with. It wasn't going to be any pleasanter today than it had been yesterday, he knew that.

Some things along the way surprised him. For one, he discovered that the road swung in along a ridge not far away and for a hundred yards or more lay in plain sight from the far side of the meadow. It struck him suddenly that Mosely might have looked down from that point and seen Silver feeding in the open. . . . If he had, that would account for his arrival so soon after Chip.

Another surprise was the tiny, parklike meadow adjoining the larger one he called his. Here, he discovered, was where the trader had camped. The road lay half a mile or more beyond, he judged; out of sight of this little clearing, at any rate. It was on the far side where he found signs of a camp, saw where several horses had been staked out to graze.

For some minutes he walked about, reading signs as clear as print to any range man. Mosely had broken camp hours ago; before daylight, apparently, and just about the time Mike had come fogging back home. Funny that Mosely hadn't missed Mike and known just where to look for him. Close together as the two camps were, it wouldn't have been any trick at all to ride over and get him before they pulled out.

"He left in a hurry—or else he kinda wanted to throw Mike back on my hands," Chip thought, puzzling over the small mystery. There was no other explanation that he could see. The trader could not have failed to miss Mike. He hadn't been burdened by any great number of horses; about fifteen or twenty head at the most. And he had helpers, as the marks of three beds attested, back in the edge of the brush.

Knuckles resting on his hips, for a long minute Chip stood there looking around him. Some things were clearing in his mind. Mosely wasn't the honest horse buyer he represented himself to be. He hadn't missed Rummy at all. He couldn't have, in that tiny clearing. He had seen Silver from the road, thought there was a chance to pick up a horse. And last night he had slipped into camp to get both horses if he could. If he had succeeded and Chip had gone after them soon enough to overtake Mosely, he'd have claimed the horses had strayed in with his bunch and he expected Chip to come after them—

"Unless he saw me first and got a chance to plant a bullet in my back," Chip finished that surmise with grim disillusionment. "I wouldn't put it past him. All that shooting down the pass wasn't just to while the time away, you can bank on that!"

And what if he had purposely turned Mike loose to back-trail to his old camp? That would give him another excuse to go prowling around—and maybe catch Chip off his guard. "He sure didn't make any noise coming into camp last night," Chip remembered. "It was when he left that I heard him." His scalp prickled at the thought. Three good horses and what money he had on him—quite a haul, if Mosely could have managed it!

"I'll just spike any excuse to try it again," he muttered, as he picked up Rummy's reins and mounted. "I'll return his horse to him *pronto*." And he added glumly, "Be like him to claim I stole Mike back. I never did like a man with eyes as close together as his are."

A little later, with all his belongings packed on Jeff and with Mike still on a lead rope, he took up the trail of the vanished trader. By long hours and fast riding, splitting the pack if necessary to give Jeff a rest and changing his saddle to Silver now and then, he thought he might overtake Mosely that night or early the next day. But he did not.

For an honest horse trader, Mosely showed a retiring disposition wholly out of keeping with his business. Where Chip had expected to see the trail cut back into the main road, the horse tracks shied off into a rocky canyon, where all tracks were lost; but not his quarry. Horse sign led him on into another gloomy ravine, down that and out into a long valley. Here he lost the trail for hours, picking it up again in a blind gulch lie never would have suspected had he not caught sight of a pair of hobbles hanging on the lowest branch of a scrubby spruce growing out of the rocks.

It might have been a deliberately placed bait, but Chip thought not. From the very first it had looked too much like a flight. Back there in camp they had gone off and forgotten a frying pan—sure sign that they had left in a hurry and in the dark; and these hobbles were too good to hang out for a sign. They had been lost, that was a cinch.

Up that gulch and down into another canyon the horses scrambled, coming out at last into a deep, rocky walled basin just as dusk was creeping in upon them. In the dark there was no hope of going on. He would have to wait for daylight or take the chance of losing himself completely. Dawn found him on the way again, sticking like a bloodhound to the trail. And if the devious windings through rough country meant anything, he could take it for granted A. B. Mosely was a mighty scared man trying to make a getaway and badly handicapped by a bunch of horses whose trail it was humanly impossible to cover.

Mosely tried hard enough. All the Indian tricks for hiding tracks he employed, and all the tricks he tried Chip guessed when he came to them. He was eight hours behind when he started, and that day he neither gained nor lost, so far as he could tell. Next day he gained a little, and the day after that he fell back a full hour, digging a mean little rock out of Mike's left front foot and then favoring him until the soreness eased somewhat. He wasn't going to deliver a lame horse over to A. B. Mosely if he could help it. He had sold a sound one. He'd return him sound.

Climbing, slipping, sliding down again. Worming through narrow ravines, wild and gloomy gorges. Crossing open country by keeping along the edge in what shelter of forest or gully could be found. Dropping back, speeding up to regain lost ground. Buzzards led him to a dead horse half eaten, brands skinned out. "As sure as God made little apples," Chip confided to Rummy, "that bunch ahead is on the dodge." That shooting down in the pass, no doubt. He wished he knew just what had happened, though it wouldn't do him any good to know.

"Horses," he said once, after riding for hours with no sound but the squeak of his saddle, the jingle of his spurs, the dull thud of shod hoofs walking among rocks—"horses, you're following an outlaw trail and I'd bet money on it." But that did not stop him; indeed, he only rode a little faster, caught the dawn at its first grayness, followed the sun farther down the west.

One thing he was determined to do. He would find Mosely if he had to ride into the Pacific Ocean to get him, and when Mosely was found, he would buy Mike back. He still had a little over a hundred dollars; he'd spend the last nickel if he had to—Mike was not going to be a night-ridden outlaw horse. Nor Rummy. Nor any horse of his. He'd put a bullet in their brains first.

Big Timber lay somewhere behind him; where, he did not know, for the trail of those horses never came within sight or sound of any human habitation. In that rough country he did not even see an Indian or a prospector. The wily timber wolves chose no more secluded way than this. What supplies he had bought in Dry Lake were nearly gone, but he dared not turn aside to buy more, lest he fail to find this trail again; nor did lie know where a store might be found. Jeff cast a shoe and went lame on the rocks, and Mike carried the depleted pack while Jeff limped clumsily along, gamely keeping up somehow. Sometimes Chip rode Silver for awhile to give Rummy a rest, though he was touchy about overtaxing the three-year-old colt. Mike he would not mount again until that bill of sale was in his possession to be destroyed.

One day late in the afternoon, he rode over a ridge and saw far down ahead of him the shine of sun on window panes. He could not be sure, but he guessed he was coming into Bozeman. Three hours later he rode into the little town and left his gaunt horses in the livery stable whose hospitable corrals looked like paradise just then.

The burr of his spur rowels on the boardwalk leading up the main street was music to his ears, lately listening to the vast silences of those empty days of solitude. The smell of steak and onions frying together, of strong hot coffee, wafted from the open window of a dingy restaurant just ahead, seemed the most delicious odor in the world.

Full-fed, trail-weary, thankful beyond words to be in a town once more, he went into the first rooming house he saw and presently was clumping upstairs and down a long and narrow hallway, following a stooped old man who bore a smoky lamp. Before he had turned to leave the musty room, Chip was sitting on the side of the sway-backed bed pulling off his boots. Shave and bath could wait. So could Mosely, until tomorrow. All hell, he told himself, couldn't stop him from sleeping twelve hours at least.

Fourteen hours went round his old silver watch. At midnight a door hinge had squealed. After a silent minute or two, broken only by Chip's slow breathing, a board under the old rag carpet squeaked. There was a faint rustling at the chair where he had left his coat and pants and his fringed leather chaps. The same board gave another squeak, the hinge a protesting squeal and the latch clicked. He lay through that and never moved a finger.

The next twelve hours held various sounds less intimate to himself. Footsteps along the hallway; a shout or two in the street below his window; at dawn the jingle of bells half-drowned in the thud of hoofs and the rattle of wheels and harness, as a freight train dragged slowly past in the dust. Chip sighed then and turned his other cheek into his soggy pillow. There were breakfast sounds in the dining room beneath his floor; odors; men talking as they clumped along the sidewalk. Other wagons went past, a dog's barking keeping pace. Later in the morning, such sounds mingled together and became the noise of a busy town. And still he slept, building new energies into his tall, tough-fibered body.

At noon someone took him by the shoulder—in his sleep he thought it was Weary—and began shaking him awake, his brown head rolling from side to side before he knew what was happening. One eye opened reluctantly, closed again.

"Here! Jar loose there. I can't wait around here all day."

"Hunh?" Chip blinked and sat up with a jerk. His eyes narrowed. One hand slid under the covers, feeling for the gun he had put there last night. It was gone. "I annexed your gun while you was dead to the world. You must have an awful gall or else you're a damn fool, to go poundin' your ear in a public place like this."

"I've got a right," said Chip, "to pound my ear wherever I damn please. What's this supposed to be, anyway? A holdup?"

"Playin' off innocent won't get you anywhere. You're under arrest, and I'd advise yuh to be kinda careful what you say. It can be used against yuh in court—if yuh get that far."

"Yes?" Chip managed to inject a good deal of sarcasm into his tone. "And what might the crime be, if it's any of my business to ask?"

"Horse stealing, for one thing. Crawl into your pants and come along. I've been settin' here an hour, waitin' for you to wake up."

"Horse stealing, hunh?" Chip repeated, and gave a snort of exasperation. "Speaking of gall, you've got the simon-pure article, I should say."

"You should say nothin'—but I s'pose you'll go ahead and talk yourself into the business end of a rope. They all do."

"I certainly will talk the other fellow in," Chip made angry retort, and reached for his clothes.

CHAPTER FOURTEEN
TROUBLE RIDES THE WIND

"We'll eat," the little man said curtly, when they came opposite the restaurant, and stood aside for Chip to enter first. "That little table over there. You set facing the wall."

The place was empty, tables set for dinner. A girl came in, walked across to them. "Why, good morning, Mr. Burns!" she said pleasantly, and looked at Chip afterwards with an inquiring smile, as if she wondered if he were prisoner or friend of the man she seemed to know.

Mind held rigidly to the business in hand, Chip ordered a meal that bespoke a conscience clear of guilt and ate it without looking up. But he knew that his every move was observed and that for the present he could do nothing about it. A man came in, glanced at their table and said, "Hello, Billy, when did you get in?" And talked a little of casual things.

Billy Burns, eh? The name seemed familiar to Chip, though he could not remember where he had heard it before. Not a bad sort of fellow, apparently. That girl seemed to like him, and the man over at the counter who was talking to Burns was friendly too. Maybe if he explained just how things stood—Burns was human, anyway.

Ten feet from the squat jail he slowed and half-turned, ignoring the gun that suddenly appeared close to his ribs.

"If you'll get that skunk of a Mosely, this thing will be straightened out *pronto,*" he said, with a forced calmness. "I'd like to talk to that jasper for about five minutes, anyway."

The gun jabbed. "Keep going, feller. You can do your talkin' inside."

With an ironic lift of the shoulders, Chip went on up the jail steps and through the door that stood open. In the office a deputy lay sprawled on his shoulder blades in a wooden armchair, his boots on the littered desk and his nose in a *Police Gazette.* He looked up, gave a welcoming bellow and swung his feet to the floor.

"Why, hello, Billy! Ain't saw you in a coon's age!" He got up, eyes coldly appraising the slim young cowboy. "Anything I c'n do?"

"Well, I'd like to borrow the use of a cell, John, if they ain't all workin'." Billy Burns pushed his gun back in its holster. "I'll be pullin' out in the morning, I think."

"Why, sure! Ain't you heard the news? You can have your pick of cells. Had a reg'lar lynchin' bee, couple of nights ago. Citizens got together and shore made a cleanin'! Took and hung five on us. Damn jail's about empty. Here's the keys—help yourself. Crazy prospector in back—don't let him out. He's plumb wild."

"Thanks, John. I'll be here for awhile. If you ain't had your dinner, now's a good time to get it."

If Burns wanted to get rid of the deputy, the big fellow took the hint. "All right, I b'lieve I will. Everybody's off chasin' stage robbers and left me holdin' 'er down alone. Brung in one bunch—them they strung up." He sent another curious glance Chip's way. "This ain't one, I s'pose?"

Burns shook his head and the deputy started off. "If that crazy feller starts in yellin', don't pay no attention," he grinned. "Gits the jimjams. Only lasts a few minutes, though."

Billy Burns waited until the deputy was down the steps. Then he locked the door and motioned to a chair. "What's this about a man named Mosely straightenin' things out?" he asked abruptly. "A feller in the pickle you're in had best come clean right at the start—or else keep his trap shut altogether. If you got things to say, now's your chance. You might not get another—not if word gets out about you bein' here."

Chip met that with a blank, uncomprehending stare. "My being here doesn't hurt anybody, unless it's Mosely," he retorted.

"What about him?"

"Why, nothing that I know of, except that I didn't steal his horse. I traded that brown and a hundred dollars for a flax-maned four-year-old he had. I gave Mosely a bill of sale and he took the horse off to his camp. That night the horse came back. Mosely didn't come after it, so I led him over there and found out Mosely had broken camp sometime in the night and left. And," he finished savagely, "I've been riding the tails off my horses ever since, trying to overtake

Mosely and turn his horse over to him. That's all, except that he saw fit to sic you onto me for a horse thief."

One booted foot swinging free, Billy Burns sat on a corner of the desk, gazing at Chip in mild meditation. "When was all this tradin'?"

"Four days ago. Away back close to the summit this side Crazy Mountain Pass."

"And you met Mosely then, or before then quite awhile?"

Chip gave a short laugh. "I met Mosely that same morning at the business end of a rifle. I caught him riding over to my three-year-old colt, Silver. He was just about to sink his loop on the colt when I pulled down on him and told him to quit it. He rode over where I was and claimed he mistook Silver for a flax-maned gelding he had, that had strayed off from the bunch." He flung out an expressive hand. "That's how I came to make the trade. He brought his horse over later—claimed he'd found him in another clearing—and I bought him. For my brown horse Mike and a hundred dollars."

"You say you gave a bill of sale for the brown. Didn't you get one with the horse you bought?"

Relief sprang into Chip's eyes. "I most certainly did." His hand moved to an inside pocket, dipped and fumbled. "That's how I knew what his name was. A. B. Mo—" His hand poised empty, darted to another pocket. The blood drained slowly from his face, surged back again. He gave Burns a straight hard look. "Since you helped yourself to it, you know as much as I do about it." His teeth clicked together, biting off recrimination.

The head under the big hat shook a slow denial. "I never saw any such paper. Somebody in that joint must of beat me to it. Your pockets was empty when I went through 'em."

Chip made sure of their emptiness now. He reached mechanically for tobacco and papers, fingers shaking so he could scarcely roll a cigarette.

"That lets me out," he said in a flat dry tone. "I've got nothing but my bare word for it. Mosely's got my bill of sale for Mike, and two fellows with him to swear to anything he says. I've got the horses."

"Two more, eh? You never said there was three in this man Mosely's outfit."

"I'm supposing there's three. I saw where three men had bedded down in the brush at his camp. Scattered out, so if one was jumped in the night the other two could get action. Saddle horses on picket ropes. Looked scaley to me. Mosely's on the wrong side of the law and I'd bank on it."

"You sure that was Mosely's camp?"

Chip looked at him over the cigarette he was lighting. "If he had a camp, that certainly must have been it. I know he followed me up the pass and was camped in the next meadow. There wasn't any other, so that had to be the one."

Billy Burns rolled a cigarette with his left hand, thoughtful eyes on Chip. "You said you never met up with him till the morning he went after your horse, and you made a trade with him."

Chip flushed. "Well, I didn't. I simply know from the way my horse Mike acted, that it was Mosely coming behind me. He had Rummy—"

"Rummy who?" With his cigarette going, Burns might have been a friend of Chip's, chinning in a bunk house—unless one looked around at the barred window.

Chip's shoulders went up. "Oh, hell, I may as well start at the beginning," he said impatiently. "The flax-maned gelding I bought is a horse I brought up from Colorado three years ago. I had the mare, Silvia, Rummy, a yearling then, and a sucking colt Silver—he's the three-year-old I've got now. Two years ago I sold the mare and Rummy to a man named Benson, out this side of Billings. My horse Mike, the brown, always was stuck on Rummy, and down in Crazy Mountain Pass he started fussing, acting like he wanted to go down to the camp below. I had to tie his head down to keep him from whinnering—"

"Afraid of visitors?" Billy Burns inquired mildly.

"Hell, no! I just wasn't in the mood for strangers butting in. Mike acted so funny, I walked down to see what was stirring him up and I saw this camp. They—"

"I thought you said you *didn't* see Mosely."

"As I was about to say," Chip coldly continued, "they had doused their fire and were sitting in the dark. I saw one when he struck a match to light a cigarette. It wasn't Mosely, but a voice like his (I know that now) bawled the fellow out for wanting to smoke. I think there was a third man, but it was too dark to see much. I went back to camp and moved my bed back into the brush. But I couldn't sleep, so when the moon came up I broke camp and pulled out."

"Kinda in the habit of travelin' at night, ain't yuh?"

Chip swallowed his anger at that thrust. "I'm a free moral agent with no strings on me, and I travel where I please, whenever it suits me," he said stiffly.

"You mean yuh *did*."

"And I will again. If I'd wanted to steal that horse back from Mosely, do you think for a minute I'd have trailed him through the most ungodly country he could find, trying to overhaul him? That in itself knocks his charge higher than a kite."

"Yeah," Burns admitted, "it would, I guess—only I never heard of this Mosely before. If you made a trade with him, I don't know a thing about it. All I know is, I've been trailing some stolen horses from Billings, and you rode one of 'em into town last night. That flax-maned gelding you call Rummy, is one I mean, and—"

"Then it *was* Mosely—"

Burns ignored the interruption. "That's the case I started out on. Now there's murder added on. Them two deputies that was on the trail twenty-four hours ahead of me—shot dead in Crazy Mountain Pass. Kinda brash to admit you was down in there about the time it happened."

Chip's face went blank with astonishment. "Two deputies killed?" He stared. "Say! I'll bet I heard the shots!"

"I bet you did too," said Billy Burns in a soft grating voice.

Chin pushed out, young Bennett leaned forward. "You're dead wrong if you think I did it. I heard the shooting just after I pulled out. Behind me, about where those fellows were squatted in the dark while their horses fed."

"And you never wondered what was taking place,— never went back to see?"

With a gesture of impatience, Chip flung out a hand. "I'm no tenderfoot," he retorted. "It wasn't my put-in and I hadn't lost any bullets."

Coldly speculating now, Burns sat and studied him. "You're slick," he summed up finally, "or you're just unlucky. You've got a smooth story, but it's damn coarse in places. Where them other four horses of Benson's are now, I don't know. But I do know you rode the flax-maned gelding into town last night, and you ain't got a thing but your bare word to show how you got hold of him."

"I sure as hell didn't steal him," flashed Chip, fighting a cold fear that was clawing at him now.

"You'd have a hard time convincin' a jury—or a mob. By your own tell, you used to own the horse. You thought enough of him to trade a good horse for him and give aa hundred dollars to boot, accordin' to you. Whoever killed them two men fogged right along up the pass, swung off the road this side the summit and camped for about twenty-four hours more or less, and then hit out over this way, following the outlaw tail that honest men never ride—"

"One did," Chip interrupted coldly, "if that's the trail I came in on."

119

"That'd make two, then. I was trailin' you up. When you swung over here into town and put up at the livery stable, you darn near give me the slip. I never thought you'd be all that bold, and it was more an accident than anything else that I run across them circus horses in the stable down beyond here. They was a dead give-away."

"You must have thought," said Chip, with a faint gleam of humor, "that the flax-maned horse had a twin all at once."

Billy Burns grinned briefly. "I did kinda think I was seem' double, there for a minute." He sobered. "But I know that four-year-old. Prince, Benson calls him. So I knew I had somebuddy I was lookin' for."

"Not me, Mr. Burns. I've told you the straight of it, far as I'm concerned. Mosely's your man. Six feet tall, I'd guess him, about forty-five, little, light blue eyes too close to his nose, and that's quite a beak. The fellow who lit a match down in the pass had his nose scratched pretty deep. Thin, dark face, lanky black hair. A bad egg, by the looks of him. They're the ones you want."

"Yeah, mebby so." Burns flipped his cigarette butt into a well-filled spittoon. "But you're the feller I've got." He stood up, looked at Chip almost sorrowfully. "Between me and you and the gatepost, that story of yours may be all true enough, but it'll git yuh about as far as a snowball goes in hell. If that's all you've got to show—"

"Let me get out after Mosely and I'll show you the men you're after."

"I'll let yuh git back into a cell and stay there till I take yuh on back to stand trial. Billings, it woulda been—but that killing was done in Sweet Grass County, so that comes first. If they don't hang yuh by law or lynchin' for murder, then you'll go on back to Billings—"

"Cheerful prospect, I must say!"

"No," Burns gravely disagreed, "it ain't a damn bit cheerful. I'm just tellin' yuh what you're up against. John Bogardus and Emery Morton, them two that was killed in the pass, have sure got lots of friends. Guilty or innocent, they'll hang the first feller drug in for that crime. I shore wouldn't want to stand in your boots, young feller, and that's a fact. You bein' caught with Benson's horse and nothin' but a cock-an'-bull story of how yuh got him, is goin' to make you look guilty as hell."

"Then what the devil—"

"Aw, come along," Billy Burns said harshly. "John Simms'll be back before long—I'll try and keep it from getting noised around what you're here for, and that's all I can do for yuh. Git yuh safe to Livingston, and yuh might have a bare chance, I dunno." With a flip of his hand he motioned.

Obediently Chip walked through the inner door and down a short corridor, Burns at his heels. His mouth had its tight-lipped stubborn look and his teeth were set so hard together the muscles lumped along his jaw. Any one of the Flying U boys would have walked warily then; but his manner was deceptively meek and Billy Burns did not know him at all.

The jail was small, with two cells on each side the corridor and another larger one across the back. This was locked and from the dusky interior issued loud and strident snoring. The other cell doors stood partly open, gruesome reminder of the death orgy staged there two or three nights before. In spite of himself, Chip felt a ripple of horror streak up his spine. Even Burns lowered his voice.

"Here's one, looks all right—" and he slid the door open as he scrutinized the bars. "Go on in—"

"Fine!" gritted Chip, and whirled and struck with his fist.

With a sigh, the little man sagged at knees and neck, slid down against the barred door. Before his head struck the dirty floor, Chip had him by the shoulders. His weight was no burden—or if it was, Chip had no consciousness of it as he carried him in and laid him on the bunk, hands folded neatly on his chest, big hat covering them. As he stood for a second looking down at the bunk while he pushed his own gun into its holster, Chip thought Billy Burns looked very peaceful.

Another minute he took to write two sentences and thrust the paper into one lax palm beneath the hat. Then he locked the cell, locked the inner door of the office, hung Billy's gun on a nail, went out and locked the jail after him, and tossed the keys back through the open, barred window with such skill that they slid under the desk out of sight.

After that, he tilted his hat over one eyebrow and cut across to a store that stood by itself; here he bought certain articles and went on to the livery stable with an armload of packages.

The stableman looked surprised to see him. "Depitty sheriff from Billings went through your stuff this morning," he said. "You meet up with him?"

Chip nodded. "Just a little case of mistaken identity. Put the saddle on the brown, there. I'm leaving the big flax-mane here, for Billy Burns. Tell him I've settled the stable bill, will you?"

So simple as that. While the jailer, John Simms, was still eating his way through a big sirloin steak, Chip Bennett rode away from the stable at an easy jog trot, Silver and old Jeff with his pack following like dogs behind him.

Even when Rummy in his stall whinnied after them, Chip did not look back. He did not dare. He was afraid that if he did he would weaken and go back and get that horse—and be the thief Burns thought him.

CHAPTER FIFTEEN

OUTLAWS AT BAY

Billy Burns came to himself, cannily lay with his eyes closed and listened. Raucous snoring from the cell next beyond him was the only sound he heard within the jail; and without, the somewhat similar plaint of a burro forgotten in a corral and wanting a drink of water. Neither sound remotely concerned himself, however, and Billy opened his eyes and saw where he was. At the first movement of his folded hands he felt the paper, but first he paused to take full cognizance of his posture, the significant way his hands were crossed one over the other, his hat nicely balanced upon his chest. It seemed to imply that he was considered a dead one so far as his erstwhile prisoner was concerned.

With a grunt he sat up, gently massaged his jaw, read the curt message:

"Going to round up Mosely. Come and get them— they're your meat."

"Hunh!" grunted Billy again, scanning each loop and curve of the carelessly perfect writing. "Pretty damn sure of himself, seems to me." And folding the note thoughtfully, he tucked it into his vest pocket and went over to try the door.

In his own way, Billy Burns was a philosopher. Once convinced that he was in that cell to stay until John Simms came and turned him loose, he made himself as comfortable as he could on the bunk and went to sleep. Chasing murderers was hard work and he needed to catch up on his rest. John would be back pretty quick now. . . .

He was wrong. Partly because of his appetite but mostly because of the pretty, blond waitress, John Simms was taking his time over the sirloin steak and what went with it. He loitered over a wide cut of raisin pie; when that was finished, he ordered a third cup of coffee, killing time until the last customer had eaten and gone, leaving him free to his courting. All told, it took him about an hour and a half to get his dinner that day, and it would have taken longer had not the boss come in to see why the girl was not carrying out the dirty dishes.

John Simms strolled down the street, then headed back to the jail. But he met a man who had been out of town and so had missed the lynching bee and now wanted all the grisly details at firsthand. The telling took some time. When Simms finally reached the jail and found it locked, he naturally assumed that Billy had finished talking to his prisoner, grown tired of waiting and had locked up and gone off—maybe hunting Simms.

So he turned back to find Billy Burns and get the jail keys. There was no sign of him on the main street, and Simms decided that the most likely place was one of the several saloons. He was a methodical man by nature. He went into the nearest, and being sociable as well as methodical, he stopped there long enough to have a drink or two with some friends and talk awhile about the lynching. He was in no great hurry, anyway. The insane prospector wasn't fed in the middle of the day.

During the entire afternoon the jailer proceeded to canvass the saloons, staying longer and longer in each one, as his search continued. Somewhere along the route he picked up a companion who insisted upon celebrating his birthday. While Billy Burns in his cell slept, awoke, waited, swore and slept again, the jailer continued his weaving journey up the street. By supper time he was too happy to be hungry and he had forgotten the object of his quest.

At nine o'clock someone came and took him by the

arm and told him he ought to go feed his prisoners, who were raising hell and wanted out. Simms was too drunk to see anything in that but a joke, and the man gave a snort and a hunch of the shoulders, and went off to his own affairs. The celebration continued uproariously until midnight, when the sheriff suddenly appeared and wanted to know what the hell was going on around there. Even so, another hour slipped along toward dawn before Billy Burns, asleep then in good earnest, was discovered in his cell and released.

That is why trouble seemed to have lost Chip's trail at the jail door and did not dog his flight out of town as he had expected it would. Counting half an hour's start, he hit a high lope back to the place where he had abandoned the telltale marks left by Mosely and his outfit, picked up the trail and followed it grimly, watching over his shoulder as he rode.

Fifteen miles or forty—how far he was behind Mosely he could only guess. Last night he knew he had gained on his quarry. But Jeff had to have that shoe replaced or he could not go on. And a man must eat and sometimes sleep. He had planned to have a blacksmith at work early in the morning, get his supplies meanwhile and hurry on—two hours of daylight lost, three at the most. Instead, he had lost nearly eight and he had Billy Burns after him like a wolf (or so he believed). But he and the horses were rested and full-fed, and though Jeff still went with one bare foot, it wouldn't take long to nail on a cold shoe. He'd keep ahead of Billy Burns, all right.

In the first sequestered spot he found, he set the shoe in place and divided Jeff's pack, giving half of it to Silver, partly to change the colt's looks. Then he pushed on, keen as a young hound on the hot scent of a rabbit. Where Mosely doubled back, riding into little rocky gulches to throw off pursuit, Chip looked ahead and gambled upon the probable objective point, cutting out such detours and picking up the trail farther on.

Toward evening the jumbled tracks of a horse herd swallowed all clues at the edge of a wide grassy flat. There he did not follow their seemingly aimless wanderings, but instead sighted a shadowed canyon almost straight across as the likeliest outlet and struck a steady gallop toward that point.

Half a mile out from its mouth he met the loose horses, grazing their way back to their favorite watering place, and grinned to himself. Mosely hadn't gained much by that trick. Up that canyon he rode as long as he could see, then walked and led the horses farther. Before dawn he was in the saddle, ready to go on as soon as it was light enough to see the ground.

Horse sign was fresher. He felt himself keener, surer on the trail. He was so sure that he forgot to look back over his shoulder, forgot the danger of showing himself against the sky when he crossed the ridges. He rode as if the world behind him was a blank and all that mattered in life lay somewhere ahead.

He topped a hill and saw beneath him another, longer valley, width narrowing at the upper end like a summer squash, pine-clad slopes and bare cliffs walling it in. Where the tracks turned aside to a tiny settlement of a scant dozen buildings he did not follow, but instead rode wide of the place and watched the ground on the farther side.

By now he knew the tracks of those horses he had followed from the summit of Crazy Mountain Pass. One overreached with a right hind foot, leaving an imprint he would recognize anywhere. A pack horse, probably, since it always traveled last in the bunch. Another had a broken calk in front. A man smoked white paper cigarettes, another rolled his in brown wheat-straw paper. There was a mule in the outfit.

Easy enough to tell when he cut sign on that bunch. His pulse raced when he picked up the trail again and knew that once more he had guessed right. With two murders and a bunch of stolen horses on their minds, they hadn't dared stop too long in that settlement, but were heading for some hide-out back in the hills. But they felt safer now. They weren't hitting so fast a pace.

Then he saw a whisky bottle lodged against a clump of weeds. He rode over and leaned and got it, and the cork was still moist in the bottle neck. A sigh of relief escaped his lungs as he tossed the bottle away and rode on. The gap was closing between himself and Mosely.

With his rifle chamber loaded and lying across his saddle, he went warily, eyes on everything that moved. Where they had struck straight out across the valley he followed at a jog trot, a casual rider to anyone who looked back and saw him. In that thick grass no dust rose to tell him where they were, but horse droppings steamed in the sun. And there was another pint flask thrown away empty. They certainly must feel safe!

Yet he would not hurry. There were three men, maybe more. And he wanted to take them back alive to Billy Burns. He had to do it or go branded as a thief and a murderer himself. Dark, he thought, would be the best time. Dark, or the last hour before dawn. With all that whisky in them, they should sleep heavily, off guard. It shouldn't be hard.

In the edge of the farther slopes they had turned north, toward the long narrow neck of the valley. They were taking their time, Chip jogging along far behind. Ten miles, fifteen—a good twenty from the little settlement. He didn't care; he had to wait for dark, anyway.

He was not surprised when the tracks turned into a used trail coming down from the hills, and his horses strung out of their own accord, sleek Silver lagging behind a little to snatch choice tips of leafy bushes as he passed. Jeff ambled along half-asleep under his full pack again—because the makeshift pack ropes had chafed Silver's belly, rubbing off the hair and raising a welt before Chip noticed it. Mike in the lead fox-trotted down the sandy trail, ears tipped forward.

Chip took the hint, lifting the rifle from his thighs as he pulled the horse down to a walk. He couldn't be certain, but it seemed to him he heard voices, though the wind blew from behind him, rustling the bushes along the trail.

Then, as the path dropped down to the flat, he heard a distant, hoarse laugh, cut through by a higher tone sharpened by fear—or it might have been fury:

"Haw-haw-haw-w! C'mon down-n!" it sounded like.

And the high voice shouting something indistin-guishable.

With a turn of the reins around the saddle horn, Chip kneed Mike forward. Why wait for dark? If this were Mosely's bunch and they were busy—

He came abruptly upon a picture he would never forget, no matter how long he lived. A low finger of ledge had blocked his view until he passed its tip and looked out across a narrow coulee mouth, no more than a hundred yards or so to the farther hill. Fifty feet up that steep slope, on a narrow shelf of rock and rubble, a magnificent black horse with a sidesaddle on it stood trembling, broadside to the hill. Its head was thrown high and it was staring down into the coulee bottom just beneath it. Behind the horse, yellow hair hanging in loosened coils on her shoulders, a slim little thing in black riding skirt stood holding a rock the size of her head upraised in her two hands, ready to throw it down upon something yet hidden from sight.

Chip urged Mike forward and saw what it was all about. On the narrow goat trail leading up to the ledge a man stood with his legs wide apart and braced against the steepness, balked for the moment of his purpose. On the level below, Mosely and another man waited on their horses, giving advice.

"You come another step and I'll brain you with this rock!"

"Aw-w, now, you wouldn't do a thing like that, wouldja?"

"Ah, come on, Fred! We ain't got time to monkey—"

"Aw-w, gwan off an' lay down!" drawled the man on

the trail, flapping a hand wearily backward. Then, wheedling again, "We wouldn't hurt yuh, girlie—honest! We just want—"

"You want your head mashed, that's what you want!" The girl lowered the rock to rest her arms, and kicked another down the steep incline. As it bounded toward him, the man swore a vicious oath and flattened himself against the hill, and laughter rose from below.

Then Mosely spoke and his voice carried a chill under its complaining whine. "Sis, we want that horse of yourn. We'll git 'im in the long run, so you might just as well make up your mind to it now and save yourself trouble. If we should have to shoot—"

"Go ahead and shoot, you big coward! You'll never get Blackie—" Pluckily she let drive with the rock, not at the man halfway up the slope but directly down upon those two who mocked and threatened from below.

With startled oaths they jumped their horses out of the way, the laughing one's mount bolting off out of the coulee. As he sat back in the saddle sawing on the reins, the man glanced aside and saw Chip riding up, looked again and seemed about to reach for his holstered gun. But he needed both hands for the horse just then, and Chip's first concern was the girl trapped on that tiny ledge; so they passed each other up for the present—to their mutual regret later on.

Mosely held in his horse and pulled his gun, waiting to see what luck the other fellow had in scrambling up the slope. He had been quick to take advantage of the girl's unguarded action. Two awkward strides brought him almost in reach of her when she dodged recklessly around beside the black horse and turned at bay, another small rock in her hand.

"You come another step and Blackie'll kick the daylights out of you!" she panted. "Go back, or I'll knock your fool head off—I will so!"

Mosely raised his six-shooter, aiming deliberately at the slight figure in her trailing black skirt. "Come down off'n there, sis, and bring your horse along, I ain't foolin' with you no longer. I'll count ten—"

"Hell, don't yuh do that, Bob," the other cried hastily. "I want that little filly m'self!"

"Ah, can the romance. We got so time fer girls!"

Rifle thrust back in its boot, Chip pulled his six-shooter and spurred forward. "Drop that gun, Mosely!" he yelled.

Like startled animals the two froze for an instant, then Mosely made a movement to obey. He knew that voice, apparently.

But the girl exploded the scene into action not foreseen. She hurled the rock down at Mosely, hitting the horse, which jumped and whirled away. Mosely fired, his bullet scorching the peak of Chip's hatcrown as it zipped past so close he felt its wind. In that same instant his own gun roared, and Mosely's horse dropped in its stride, throwing its rider heavily upon the rocky ground.

The man on the slope reached for his gun. But another rock came bouncing down at him, caught him off guard with his eyes on Chip, swept his feet from under him and sent him down the steep hillside to an abrupt stop against a boulder.

While he was scrabbling to get up, Chip made a flying leap upon him. The gun he kicked into a bush. He slammed the fellow's head back against the rock, yanked off his dirty neckerchief and did an expert job of tying, letting the feet wait for the moment.

As he turned to slash off saddle strings with his hunting knife, Mosely lifted himself to a half-sitting posture and leveled his gun. As if wrestling a calf, Chip flung himself upon the man—and into the path of a rock aimed at Mosely. Shooting stars laced across his vision then, but he hung on doggedly to his task.

Not until Mosely was tied hand and foot with leather from his own saddle did Chip stand up and lift his eyes to the ledge. The girl stood there, staring down at him, a rock held ready in each small fist.

CHAPTER SIXTEEN
ALL IN THE DAY'S WORK

"Well," he said frostily, when the silent stare could hold no longer, "you can come on down, now."

The wind blew strands of corn-yellow hair across the girl's face and she brushed it aside with one shoulder, still clinging to her rocks. At the back of her neck a starched sunbonnet dangled by its tied strings. Her black calico riding skirt was earth-stained, blowing and flapping with little popping sounds, like clothes on a line. Even from where he stood fifty feet below her he could see she was panting with fear or rage, or both.

And the sweaty horse behind her stood with quick-pal-pitating flanks, sign of the long race he had run.

But Chip was wary of girls. Trouble-makers, every one he had ever known. His artist eyes drank in the picture those two made, but emotionally he braced himself for resistance. Fellows like Cal Emmett, always getting mashed on a girl, made him sick. And a man like the one at his feet ought to be hung up by his heels. The look in her eyes, as if she expected him to act the skunk too, made him feel like crawling on his horse and riding off without another word. But he couldn't do that. She'd got herself into a jackpot where she needed help.

The ice of his resentment hardened his next attempt. "I said you can come on down."

"Like fun I will!"

"Suit yourself." He shrugged eloquent shoulders. "Maybe you belong on the shelf, but your horse won't stand there forever." Mechanically he reached for the makings, then remembered his manners and let his hand drop away from his pocket. "Far be it from me to hurry you any, but I might point out that these two worthies are not in a position to bother you again."

She continued to stare. "Maybe they're not, but you are. You needn't think I'm fooled. You're one of the bunch."

Chip's gaze narrowed. "Yes?" He glanced down at Mosely, then back up at her. "I don't see where you got that idea."

"You called that one by name, anyway."

"Oh." He bit back a smile. "I also performed a little

tying act that you'd hardly call friendly—and you'll notice he wasn't exactly cordial when I showed up."

With her lifted shoulder she again brushed hair out of her eyes. "Oh, you're on the outs—but all the same, I'm not trusting anybody today, thank you."

Chip sat back upon the boulder, crossed his feet and pushed his hat back so the brim wouldn't hide her from him. He gave her a better chance to study his thin good-looking face and to see the wave in his thick brown hair (no girl ever imagines a villain with nice wavy hair), but he did not know that he was letting his good looks and his youth speak for him.

"You'll have to figure out some way of getting your horse down off that ledge," he observed, eyes on the sifting of tobacco into a cigarette paper. Not polite, maybe, but if she were going to be so darned ornery he might as well smoke. "You'll have to tackle the job eventually, so why not now?"

From under his straight dark eyebrows he saw her head turn for an uneasy glance at the narrow shelf where they stood. While he rolled and smoothed the cigarette, twisted the end and found a match and lighted it leisurely on the warm rock, cupped palms around the blaze, and saw the blue thread of smoke rise and whip away on the wind, he let the girl consider the full awkwardness of her position.

"If you try jumping him off, he'll break his neck," he continued, in the detached tone he could make so maddening. "If you try to turn him around, he'll fall off—ditto. He can't go on up—not unless you can produce wings for him; even a mountain goat would count ten before he tackled that job. So—"

"I wish you'd mind your own business."

"Nothing," said Chip, "could suit me better. I hope you don't think I'm hanging around here for fun. When you and your horse are down and safely headed for home, I'll attend to my own business. It's pretty important—to me, at least." Then some look in her eyes thawed him to friendliness. "My job is to take these men back to stand trial for murder. So if you'll make up your mind to come down from there and let me go up and see about the horse—"

She dropped the rocks and lifted her riding skirt daintily at the sides, holding it against the tug of the wind. "There used to be a trail up here," she said in a harassed tone. "It was a shortcut over into Laughing Water Coulee. There must have been a slide or something—and I didn't know. When those men chased me and ran off the horses I was taking home, I started up the trail to get away from them. And it peters right out to nothing, here. Blackie just barely stopped himself in time."

She looked all at once little and scared and ready to cry. Her defiance had melted under his voice, his slimness and good looks, his youth. She saw him now for what he was, let him see her helplessness. "There's another one, remember. He'll come back—"

"If he does, he won't hurt anything." It was less a statement than a promise.

"He might—while you're busy with Blackie." She was coming down, picking her way through the rubble on the steep fragment of trail. The horse swung his head around to watch her questioningly, and she stopped and looked at him with sober gray eyes. "I don't see how on earth you'll get him down from there," she said irrelevantly, as if the third outlaw mattered less after all than the horse.

"You watch my smoke," Chip said lightly, though it was not his habit to boast.

When she was down beside him he saw how small she was, how appealing her long-lashed gray eyes, her quivering red mouth with its droop at the corners. She could have stood under his outstretched arm without touching—he put the thought sternly from him. Pretty time to be thinking of a girl's looks, with all the trouble he had on his hands!

He walked over and got Mosely's gun and gave it into her hands. "Anything you don't like the looks of, you won't have to throw rocks," he said brusquely. "You're heeled."

"Thanks. I can shoot, but Mamma won't let me have a gun. She thinks it isn't—nice for a girl."

Chip snorted. "It's a heap nicer than to be caught without one sometimes. You keep that. You've earned it, I guess."

Mosely swore viciously at that, whereupon Chip gagged him with a red handkerchief badly in need of washing, yanked his hat down over his eyes and left him, to do the same by the other, who was just beginning to show signs of life. "They won't bother you," he said shortly, and went calmly about the next job, uncomfortably conscious of the girl's clear gaze following his every movement.

A ticklish proposition, the best he could make of it. He could see well enough how the girl had got into such a jam, but that didn't help a darned bit now. A part of the ledge had sluffed off, probably when the slide carried away the trail beyond it. Now it was so narrow there was barely room to stand alongside the horse. Looking down from the dizzy perch, he was amazed at the pluck of the girl, standing up there in that long skirt, fighting off those two so-and-so's with rocks. It was the grittiest thing he had ever seen. But what kind of folks did she have, that would let her ride around alone and take such chances?

But that didn't cut any ice now. Lucky for her he'd happened along when he did. Lucky for him too, maybe; he had two of the skunks and he'd get the other one, all right. But this—a devil of a job he'd staked himself to!

"Do you think you can get him down all right?" the girl called up anxiously.

"First four miles are the rockiest," Chip made cryptic reply. His hands were patting, rubbing, soothing the frightened animal as he spoke. The horse seemed to know the danger; he was sweating, trembling like an old man with palsy. His breath came in gusts, flaring his nostrils. Eyeballs stared so a white rim showed.

"How is he on backing up?" Chip asked over his shoulder, forced cheerfulness in his voice.

"Not very good, I'm afraid. I thought of that, but it's so narrow—He's awful smart, though. If he knew it was for his good—"

"I'd tell a man it's for his own good!"

"Tell Blackie, why don't you?" she asked slyly, with her first gleam of humor. "He's smarter than lots of men."

"You can't tell a horse anything while he's walling his eyes at old lady Trouble," Chip answered, grinning in spite of himself. "Blackie's got his own ideas about this business."

But he proceeded to change those ideas, give Blackie something else to think about. Adroitly, while he rubbed and patted, he blindfolded the horse with his neckerchief, talking all the while in that soothing undertone his own horses knew so well. He did not hurry, though with that third outlaw ranging loose, he knew there was need of haste. He did not let the horse suspect there was any ticklish job to be done, and so the terrified quivering of Blackie's muscles quieted, his head drooped a little, braced legs relaxed.

And while he continued to talk, Chip began gently pressing the horse backwards, with his own body shielding it from the sheer drop off the ledge. Five feet, ten feet, fifteen—they were off the shelf and into the narrow trail that pitched steeply down through treacherous shale and rubble. A goat track. No rider would ever attempt that climb unless he were desperate—as the girl must have been. No horse could have made it, save a sure-footed animal in full gallop, carried upward by excitement and in the momentum of his stride.

It looked impossible, but it had to be done. One misstep might send the horse rolling as the outlaw had rolled. One loose stone turning under a foot—and Chip was on the downhill side, hands and voice keeping the horse in what trail there was.

Slow. One step backward, seconds spent in rubbing the salt-streaked shoulder. One more step, waiting until all four hoofs stopped scrabbling for a foothold and stood quiet.

"Down—Steady, boy—take your ti-ime—nothing to get snorty about. Hell of a note, asking a horse to back down off a bluff like this, but we've just got to do it, old socks. Back—that's the stuff! Nothing's going to hurt yuh—not a damn—thing. You just have to come off your perch, that's all. You can't turn mountain goat all at once, y' see. Plumb foolish to try.

"Back a little more, boy. Little more—careful of that rock—little more—keep your rump close to the wall— like that. That's fine! Oh, there's nothing to get skittish about—you leave it to me. Don't like it such a lot, hunh? Whoa, boy. Straight back. This thing of turning on a dime is all right, and nobody claims you couldn't do it—only this dime happens to be standing on edge, see? 'Fraid you couldn't cut the mustard.

"All right, now, let's try it once more. Back, boy. Careful—no rush. Ah, that's just a rock rolling down." And he patted and soothed, while the small avalanche slid in its own dust to the bottom. "Steady, boy! Nothing's going to hurt yuh—not if I know myself. I'm looking after yuh now—don'tcha know it, hunh? You go tromping around here by guess and by gosh, and you're liable to bust a leg. That wouldn't do, now, would it? You bet your life it wouldn't; wouldn't do *atall*."

He had forgotten the girl watching him from below; forgotten those two tied and gagged, with their hats pulled over their eyes. Forgotten also for the moment was that third man who had forged past him sawing on the reins of a stampeding horse. For the moment, life had drawn in to a focus there on that coulee wall, its only duty the safe landing of that scared black horse on the level ground below.

CHAPTER SEVENTEEN
BILLY BURNS AGAIN

He did it. Did it in ten minutes that had seemed to stretch out into an eternity of strained effort, of fighting with voice and touch the panic of a high-strung horse.

When he pulled off the blindfold at last, down at the foot of the hill, Chip's body was so wet with sweat his shirt stuck to his back. His knees wanted to buckle under him; did buckle, so that he sat down abruptly on the boulder to save himself from falling. His arm shook when he lifted it to wipe the beads of perspiration off his face—shook so he would not attempt to roll a cigarette, much as he needed a smoke.

He knew the girl had run to the horse, but he did not look at her. He was also completely unaware that while he was performing that nightmare task up there a man had ridden quietly across the coulee's mouth and dismounted, watching every move he made. Keen as it usually was, his instinct failed to let him know that the man stood there now a few feet behind him, still watching him quizzically.

So his heart jumped and skipped three beats when the drawling voice he had last heard in the Bozeman jail remarked, quizzically:

"Looks like you've been kinda busy around here. Got yourself a coupla men and then tried fly-walkin' on a cliff for a change. Ain't yuh never goin' to quit and settle down?"

While he took one quick, tight breath Chip did not move.

"You made good time," he said coolly then, and reached for the makings. "You must have left right after I did."

"No-o, you had a head start, all right." Billy Burns moved around and stood beside Mosely's long quiet figure. "I happen to know this country. Used to work over here. I knowed where you'd come out, so I cut acrost country."

He glanced at the man stretched before him, looked at Chip. "You sure believe in bein' thorough," he observed laconically.

"Not as thorough as you might think." Chip blew a thin ribbon of smoke through tightened lips. "Take a look, why don't yuh? That's Mosely."

"The dickens it is!" Billy Burns lifted the hat, stared into eyes as coldly malignant as a snake's. "Slick Robbins is the only name I ever knowed 'im by. Thought you was doin' time down in Wyoming, Slick."

He had twitched off the gag. The stream of blasphemous epithets that gushed forth was astounding. He leaned again and delivered a stinging slap across the evil mouth.

"There's a lady present," he grated, sending an oblique glance toward Chip, who had started for Mosely.

Chip sat down again, eyes watching every move as Billy replaced the gag and turned to the other captive.

"This feller I don't know," Burns observed thoughtfully. "Don't have to. Any friend of Slick's is bad as they make 'em." This time he made no move to remove the gag, but turned and looked keenly at the young man sitting there calmly on the boulder. "You said there was three in the bunch. Whereabouts is the other one?"

It was the girl, standing with both arms around Blackie's neck, who answered him. "The other one's horse stampeded when this gentleman rode up and started shooting," she said. "He went off that way—" swinging one arm toward the valley "—but I remember now, I saw him coming back, cutting in behind that rocky point. They ran off a bunch of our horses, Mr. Burns, up this coulee. They had a bunch of their own they were driving along, and I was hazing our horses in off the flat. I had them strung out toward home, so I was sort of taking my time and poking along at a walk—"

"How long ago was this?"

"Oh, it seems as if it must have been hours ago, so much has happened," she exclaimed. "But I suppose it really wasn't more than fifteen minutes or so before this gentleman showed up."

Billy Burns looked at Chip. "Know how long you been here?"

"Like the young lady, a good deal happened in a very short time. Not over half an hour; probably less."

Billy Burns rubbed his chin thoughtfully. "That's about right. If his horse bolted when the shootin' started, and he had to pull him down and then swing back, he ain't got far. They was headed up this coulee, yuh mean, Mary?"

"Yes. I rode into a swale, out there in the valley, and got off to pick some flowers—they're up there on that horrible ledge right now. I didn't see anyone at all till I came up on level ground again, and then I saw three riders swing out from this coulee and haze our saddle bunch in with theirs, and run them up in here. They didn't see me then, I guess. So I took in after them—"

"Ain't your dad learned you any better than that?"

"Well, but I thought maybe they didn't know anyone was with the horses. The country's overrun with horse thieves and outlaws, but our stuff has always been left alone, for some reason. You know that, Billy."

"Yeah, sure I know that. Too close to their hide-out. It's policy to do their dirty work farther away from home."

"Anyway, I wasn't going to let them run all our broke horses off without lifting a finger to stop them. I chased them on up the coulee quite a ways. And then they saw me coming and they turned around and came after me."

"Did, hunh?"

"They scared me, the way they acted. They chased

144

me clear back down here, and—so I tried to cut up over the hill and get Papa and Barney. I got up part way, and there wasn't any trail, any more."

"There never was," Billy Burns made dry comment.

"There was a kind of a one. Papa rode up there once," the girl defended her foolhardiness. "Anyway, I couldn't get up or down, and they were down here and I was standing them off with rocks, and this gentleman came along."

"Are you sure that third man cut back up the coulee?"

"Yes, I saw him ride behind that point of rocks right after this one fell downhill. He was either going back the way they all came up the valley, or he was taking that old trail that cuts down into this coulee up about a mile from here."

"He never went back," Burns declared, "or I'd have met him. If he took that old trail—"

Chip smoked a cigarette that had no flavor. What was Burns stalling for? Why didn't he quit this granny talk and send the girl on home? He wasn't fooling anybody, playing cat-and-mouse like that. When he got good and ready, he'd disarm his third prisoner— and the girl would be hanging around to watch the proceeding.

On a sudden impulse, he dropped his cigarette, ground it under his heel. And before anything less swift than a bullet could stop him, he had Mike's reins in his hand and had flung himself into the saddle.

And then he knew that he wouldn't—simply because it was not in him to do it. He couldn't gallop off up that

145

coulee and dodge back on the old trail the girl spoke about, pick up Silver and Jeff and hit for the hills. It could have been done. Burns would have thought he was obligingly going to catch another outlaw for him. But it didn't work out. He looked at the girl standing there beside her horse and knew that he couldn't turn tail and run from that leather-faced little deputy sheriff she seemed so friendly with. Hell, he wasn't a quitter, he hoped!

All in a flash his thoughts went racing, while Billy Burns stood there hipshot, thumbs locked inside his belt, a peculiar expression on his face.

"Before you go hellin' off after them horses and the feller that stole 'em," Billy said, with mild urgency in his tone, "yuh better let me deputize yuh and stake you to a badge. I got an extry one I ain't usin'—you might as well have it. Give yuh authority to take them horses wherever yuh find 'em." He walked toward Chip. "Otherwise, somebuddy that's honest might buy in, thinkin' you're a horse thief."

Astonishment held Chip motionless on his horse. His startled glance flicked Billy Burns' face and moved on to meet the girl's steadfast, bright gaze upon him.

That glance she answered. "Yes, why don't you do that? If Billy Burns wants to make an officer of you, it's because he needs you and—trusts you to make good. And I've got to get those horses back! If I don't, Papa never would let me out of sight of the house again."

"And a darned good thing if he didn't," Billy Burns added severely. He went and stood close to Chip, lowering his voice so that Mary would not hear.

"Slick Robbins bein' in the country and foggin' over here with a coupla men and a bunch of horses kinda puts a new face on things," he said. "Checks up with your story. Puts you in the clear, far as I can see."

"Glad you woke up to that fact," slipped out before Chip could stop it.

"Oh, I ain't so slow as a rule. Way things stand, it's split into two jobs. Slick Robbins I'd hate to trust outa my sight—don't know the other one, but the fact he's teamin' with Slick proves a plenty."

"Slick was going to shoot her. That other skunk wanted her—alive," Chip muttered between close teeth.

Billy Burns nodded. "I wouldn't put nothin' past 'em. Well, the way you took hold here, I guess you're pretty tol'able safe to hold your own most anywhere. You go round up that feller and haze them horses back, and I'll take charge of the prisoners. Any reason why you don't want to tell your name?" His brown eyes bored into Chip's.

"None in the world. It's Bennett. Chip Bennett."

"Hm-m—Flyin' U outfit, up north of the Missouri, hunh?"

Blood surged into Chip's face. "That's neither here nor there."

"No-o, I guess not. Well, I happen to be a United States marshal, though mighty few folks know that. I work outa Billings, just as a deputy sheriff, far as the public is concerned. For reasons of my own. But I've got jurisdiction, even over here."

While Chip sat in the saddle, not knowing what to say, Billy Burns fumbled in a pocket, brought up a small plain-looking badge and offered it as if it were something especially important; which it was.

"I guess I ain't makin' any mistake," he said gravely. "Any kid like you that can slam me into a cell and lock me in so good it takes the half of Bozeman to git me out, can handle himself most anywhere."

"I had to. I—"

Billy Burns talked right on through the interruption. "This deputizes you for special work, and that's to round up that third man and bring him over to Laughin' Water; that's the next coulee above this one. I'll take Slick and his pardner over there—and if Babe Allison's home, I'll leave 'em with him and come on back and meet yuh. If not, you bring 'im along, anyway. Alive, if you can make it."

Chip found his voice. "You don't have to make an officer of me just for a little job like that," he said stiffly, to hide his shamed gratitude.

"Hell, I don't *have* to do anything," beamed Billy. "Maybe it ain't as triflin' a job as what you expect. If that jasper seen his two cronies laid out over here, it's likely he kep' right on goin'. He woulda picked you off like a blackbird on a fence rail if he'd saw you up there with that black horse. That goes to show he was high-tailin' it away from here."

"Well," Chip rashly pointed out, "I managed to over-haul him once when he had a bigger start than this. I ought to be able to do it again."

"Yeah, I s'pose yuh had. And the sooner, the quicker.

That badge, young feller, is to kinda show where you stand."

"Oh." From under his tilted hatbrim, Chip stole a glance at the girl. Mary Allison. Pretty name—but not half as pretty as she was, with her expectant face across which her corn-yellow hair kept blowing.

He undid a button of his shirt and pinned the badge on the underside of the facing, feeling her eyes upon him, knowing she was smiling. He looked up, saw that he was right, tipped his hat with a shy formality.

"I'll be back *pronto*," he said, and touched Mike with the spurs.

He did not ride up the coulee but across to the finger of rock. Jeff and Silver had been left there when he dashed across to the hill. Somehow it had never occurred to him to wonder why they hadn't poked their noses around that point before now. But they were pretty well trained, come to think of it. Times before, when he had spurred ahead in what seemed an unwarranted burst of speed, those two had simply waited and grazed philosophically until he went back after them or whistled them up to where he waited.

They'd done that now, he told himself uneasily. But though he rode back along the trail a little way and whistled his old call, no head lifted above the bushes to neigh the accustomed answer.

There were tracks. The deep-scored prints of a horse in full gallop, the marks printed over here and there by the shod hoofs of Billy Burns' horse. There were other tracks that looked like Jeff's and Silver's; Jeff's he knew by the stamp of that unshaped shoe he had nailed on. They had turned in the trail and started back—following those other hoofprints.

Frowning, he followed a little way to where the old trail turned off into the hills, saw them there before him.

With a quick yank, Chip pulled his hat down more firmly on his head, ready to ride against the wind—and ride hard. He knew now what had happened. That third outlaw had spotted his horse, swung back and thrown his loop on Silver. Maybe he had been willing to let the pack horse stay, but Jeff was too damned loyal to his bunch. Where Silver went, Jeff would follow.

Rummy in strange hands had been bad enough, but Silver—Chip's jaws came together with a snap. His heels came back, jabbing Mike's tender flanks with his big rowelled spurs. The chase was on now in deadly earnest.

CHAPTER EIGHTEEN

THE FLYING U HEARS THE TRUTH

The Flying U roundup was delayed for a day in its camp on Deep Creek, just where it enters the breaks at the edge of the Badlands. Moreover, they were not riding the range as might have been expected, but instead were morosely spreading their blankets and quilts (or corner wads, or soogans, as they were more likely to call them) on sagebrush to dry. For the night had been a wild and a wet one, with the roar of wind and the crash of thunder, and with lightning streaking through the deluge of rain that swept aslant up the river bottom.

The night hawk had ridden for ten miles, trying to keep his horses in sight, and only within the last hour had he succeeded in getting them back and into the rope corral. Patsy the cook had exhausted his Germanic vocabulary and the patience of the crew before breakfast was ready, and the Happy Family was practically ready to follow the advice which the devil gave job, and curse God and die—figuratively speaking. For the tent had come down on them in the night, and wet canvas slapping and ballooning about a man's head in a hard, cold wind is a thing no man can take with a smile; and getting that same tent up again was no joke, either. Nor did the makeshift breakfast help their tempers much.

It was into this atmosphere of bleak discomfort that Steve Duncan rode cheerfully, pancakes of doby mud sticking to his horse's feet as he plodded up the flat. It was that cheerfulness which struck the Happy Family as unnatural and caused them to ask him what Santy had brought him. At least, Cal Emmett asked that question, which expressed the unanimous thought of the others.

"Well, it's Santy I come to see," Steve told him, grinning. "Me and Bob got him a little present, and Bob, he got cold feet when it come to makin' a speech and givin' it to him, so I just brought it over."

He swung down from his horse, questing glances sweeping the camp, as he sauntered over and sat himself down on a box. "You had some rain last night, looks like," he remarked unnecessarily. "Didn't hit Flying U creek at all. Bob and me stayed at the ranch last night, gettin' it in shape to turn over."

This, of course, was all Greek to the Happy Family, who looked at one another inquiringly. At the last sentence, J. G. came out of the mess tent and stopped before Steve.

"Who you turning your ranch over to, Steve? Somebody buy you boys out?"

It was Steve's turn to stare. He gave a short, puzzled laugh. "Well, yes. An outfit up that way, called the Flyin' U, bought us out. For cash. Right slap up against your east line, so yuh want to look out for 'em." His tone changed as he met J. G.'s blank look. "Ain't Chip told yuh yet? It was Dunk Whittaker bought us out. Chip—he kinda made the deal."

J. G. brought out his old pipe without knowing what motions his hands went through. "When was this?"

"Oh—le'see. Sunday's a week—and las' Sunday Bob got back from Helena—just about twelve days ago, Chip started out to git things done." He looked up from the cigarette he was rolling, his eyes meeting Weary's intent gaze. "You mind that day you come down to camp lookin' for him? Well, that's the day he went in to talk turkey to Dunk."

"What for?" J. G. snapped the question in before Weary could speak.

"Well, seems like Chip had got wise to something Dunk had in mind for us boys. Nothin' much—little charge of beef rustlin'. Dunk wanted to break us or drive us out. You know that, J. G."

152

"I know I wouldn't stand for anything underhand," J. G. snapped again.

"Sure not. We knowed that, all along. Chip knowed it too. Way I figure, he was afraid you'd be pulled into something that was goin' to make a big stink, if the facts ever got out. So he gits him what proof he thinks he needs, jumps a train and goes to see Dunk—"

"Is that where he was when we was lookin' for him?"

Steve looked slightly surprised, eyeing J. G., while with his tongue tip he moistened the paper edge and pressed it down smooth, rounding the cigarette neatly.

"Why, yes, I s'pose maybe he was. Sure, it was. Chip's so damn close-mouthed—Well, anyway, he brought back the deed for us to sign and Bob, he took it back and got the money. Bob, he took a pasear down around Billings, lookin' things over and seein' what the outlook is around there for gittin' a little place. But I dunno. He didn't run acrost what he wanted—"

When his cigarette was going, he glanced again around the silent group. "Where's Chip at? I got that little present for 'im that Bob bought."

The Happy Family moved uneasily. "He ain't here right now," Weary told Steve vaguely. "If it's anything I could—"

"Sure! You give it to him, Weary, when he comes. Chip's kinda funny. He hates to take favors from anybody. Damn near jumped down Bob's throat when Bob wanted to give him something on the deal. But if you take and hand this to 'im, and just say it's a little present from Bob and Steve—"

From an inside pocket he drew a flat case of dark

blue plush, wrapped in a single page of an old magazine. The wrapping came off in his hands, as the Happy Family crowded up to see.

"Bob wanted to buy him a watch," he said, almost apologetic. "But hell, he knowed Chip never would carry it; not as long as he's got that watch that used to be his dad's. So he hunted around and got him the best damn watch chain and charm there was in the hull town. Beaut, hunh?"

"Mamma!" Weary exclaimed, as hatcrowns drew together over the opened case. "Real diamonds, I bet."

"You're damn tootin' they're real diamonds. Five of 'em. And lookit on this side. Them's rubies. Way Bob come to buy it, the man in the joolrie store had this made to order for a big gambler in town. And then the feller got cleaned and shot the other feller and they throwed him in jail; so the jooler, he was willin' to knock off some on the price.

"And lookit here. It's a locket, where you c'n keep a lock of your girl's hair—somep'n like that. Purty slick, hunh? You tell Chip there ain't another watch charm like that in the world, fur as we know. And take a look at this, once. C. B. monogram; Chip's initials carved on the back. That was Bob's idea."

"Well, whadda yuh know about that!" Weary enthused in a hollow tone, which he could not for the life of him make hearty.

The case passed from hand to hand, that all might look and lift the chain to feel how heavy it was— because it was solid gold nuggets hooked together with gold wire, Steve explained. And if the Happy Family

154

had less to say than usual, Steve probably assumed that for once in their lives they were completely flabbergasted with so much magnificence. The nuggets, he went on to say, were some the gambler had been saving for years, picking them up here and there around the mining camps and waiting until he had a matched string of them; matched as to weight and size, though the shape varied considerably. Each was about the size of a navy bean before it has been in water, and the whole thing was heavy.

"Course," he admitted, when the ornate gift had returned to Weary's hands, "Chip won't maybe feel like wearin' it common—"

"He sure as hell won't have no trouble keepin' his vest down to his pants, when he hooks that in a buttonhole," Cal Emmett made envious comment. "Make him hump-shouldered packin' it around."

"Take a block an' tackle to hoist 'im on a horse, by golly!" Slim enlarged upon the idea.

They were talking to cover their remorse—hide it even from themselves; but Steve could not know that and their remarks nettled him a little.

"Well, by gosh, if it was forty rod long with a diamond big as your thumb every six inches, it wouldn't wipe the slate off of what we feel we owe Chip," he declared, with some heat. "Way Dunk had it framed with Pete Riser, and I don't know who all besides, me and Bob both would 'a' been railroaded to the pen and all hell couldn't 'a' saved us. That—of a Pete Riser was packin' in beef to our camp and claimin' he bought it or traded deer meat—got it off them nesters over here

155

on Dog Creek. And all the time he was killin' Flyin' U beef by Dunk's orders and plantin' the hides where it would look like we done it."

"You got proof of that?" J. G. demanded sternly.

"Proof enough to know the hull scheme. Chip heard 'em talkin' in town. He didn't know who they was framin', but he made it his business to find out. All on the quiet. Then he went down and jumped Pete about it, and got enough outa him so he had 'em both where the hair was short. And before Pete could git to Dunk, Chip, he beat it to Helena and—well, puttin' two and two together, Dunk made out our deed in front of Chip's gun."

"He never said—"

"'Course not. He didn't want me and Bob to say nothin' about it, either. We didn't, till Dunk come through with ten thousand for the ranch. Bob told him we'd start us up a ranch somewheres else, so we're pullin' out quick as we can git shaped up. And I wish you wouldn't let on to Chip like I told yuh. I wouldn't want him to git sore. Or Dunk, either. Between you and me, Dunk's had his little lesson, and I don't guess he'll ever try and pull anything like that again."

He looked at the nugget chain and returned to his defense of its barbaric splendor. "But if you think that's spreadin' it on too thick, put yourselves in our place a minute. There we was, not knowin' a thing about it—just waitin' like sagehens to be knocked over with a club. Chip saved our bacon for us—and yours too, J. G. We got too many friends in the country for Dunk to git away with a frame-up like that, claimin' it was the Flyin' U done it.

"And Chip wouldn't take nothin' like money—" His honest eyes swept the group. "It's about all we can do for 'im," he said, his voice troubled. "It's all Bob could find that come anywhere near—"

Weary came warm-heartedly to the rescue then. "I don't know of anything that would fill the ticket any better. It sure is a peach. Chip is going to be proud to death when he sees it. He's been tryin' to save up enough money to get himself a nice watch chain—ain't he, boys?"

"Sure has," half a dozen voices testified with convincing haste.

Slim bettered that. "Why, just the other day, by golly—day b'fore we pulled out from the ranch, it was—Chip was huntin' through the catalogue, pickin' one out for himself. They was one he wanted bad," he expatiated, goggle eyes on Steve, "but it cost around twenty-five dollars, and Chip he couldn't hardly afford—"

"This here chain and charm," Steve broke in, "set Bob back just exactly six hundred dollars! The jooler th'owed in the nuggets, 'cause the feller that ordered it, he furnished them hisself."

"Mamma!" breathed Weary in a whisper.

That amazing bit of information off his mind, Steve turned to his horse. "Well, I got to be siftin' along. Told Bob I'd git home time he did and help load up the wagon. We're goin' to start trailin' our cattle out—up into Valley County somewheres, chances are."

His hand touched a leather case tied alongside the

157

horn. "Oh, yeah. Here's somep'n else Bob got for Chip. That was before he seen that watch chain. Pair of field glasses he thought maybe Chip might like. They're little, but oh, my! You can see to knock a fly off a horse's rump down in Texas, damn near. Binocallers, they call 'em. Some kinda foreign glasses that's got the regular kinda field glasses skinned a mile." He grinned with boyish pride. "Chip's name's stamped on 'em, so none of you highbinders can git away with 'em accidental."

They stood and looked at him, not finding anything to retort.

"Here, Weary. You take and give 'em to Chip. And tell 'im me and Bob both says thanks till he's better paid."

"I sure will, Steve." Weary stood with the gifts in his two hands and watched Steve ride away, angling up toward high ground where the sandy soil made better going. "I—sure—will," he repeated slowly under his breath, almost as if he were making a vow.

CHAPTER NINETEEN
WEARY PICKS UP CHIP'S TRAIL

"Any of you boys know where Chip went to?" It was the first time J. G. had mentioned his name since that night nearly two weeks ago when frayed nerves had betrayed the outfit into so much bitterness. His shrewd gray eyes moved accusingly from face to face.

"His tracks was pointed toward Dry Lake," Jack

Bates said, with a quick sidelong glance at his fellows. "He went up over the hill and off north. I saw where he turned into the Dry Lake trail—"

"He was in buyin' a grubstake that night, Jimmy told me," Shorty supplied further information. "Didn't have much to say,—cut Jimmy off pretty short, from all I could gather. He was in at Rusty's place, but he didn't stay more'n a few minutes. Rode on outa town. Nobody saw him after that."

"Aw, I betcha he's went to Canada," Happy Jack declared, with his usual pessimism. "We won't never see him no more."

"Chances is he went on back down where he come from," Shorty suggested. "Wyoming or Colorado—down there somewhere."

With his handkerchief, Weary was carefully wrapping up the blue velvet case. "I'll damn soon find out," he stated, more curtly than they had ever heard him speak before. "Sorry, J. G., but I guess you'll have to look for another man to take my place. Roundup or no roundup, I'm going to find Chip."

"Well, tell 'im to git back here on the job and quit rangin' around like a homesick dogie. He's on the payroll and he might as well be makin' a hand. You tell 'im I said so." And J. G. turned abruptly and walked off to the horse corral, where he stood biting hard on his pipe and staring at horses he didn't see at all.

That is why Weary rode out of the Flying U camp no more than fifteen minutes behind Steve Duncan, with more than a thousand dollars' worth of watch chain in his pocket, as complete a camp outfit as could be rolled inside a blanket tied behind his cantle, and the avowed determination that he'd come back with Chip Bennett riding alongside him or he wouldn't come at all.

It is only just to say that to a man the Happy Family would have gone with him, had that been possible, and that only hard necessity kept J. G. from going along. Though it is also true that nothing of the sort was so much as hinted by any one of them.

Weary headed south, crossed the river and made cautious inquiries at Cow Island settlement. What kinda time had Chip made with his pack outfit? That is, what time of day had he shown up at Cow Island?

Chip, it appeared, had not shown up at any time, which made Weary wonder if he had traveled north after all. He didn't think so. His hunch was to continue south.

At Roundup, on the Musselshell, the entire population of two persons remembered the young fellow with the pack horse and the silver-maned (or flax) three-year-old trailing loose behind. They remembered him chiefly because he had gone straight on past without stopping. No, they didn't know as they could say just what day that was.

At Billings Weary stayed overnight, partly to make careful inquiries and partly because he needed a good sleep and a square meal or two. Like Chip, when he reached Bozeman, Weary was dead tired from the pace he had set himself, and he had skipped altogether too many meals.

In spite of that, he made the rounds of all the saloons, asked at the different livery stables, had all the storekeepers searching their memories for a tall young fellow who might have bought camp grub—pack horse supplies—a week or so ago. They ought to remember; customers who meant to pack their supplies on a horse had no liking for paper bags—

Every storekeeper who sold food supplies in that town tried to help Weary, but the trouble was that too many tall young men had bought camp supplies in that town within the past two weeks. Which was only natural at that time of year, when travel was always at its height.

The trail seemed utterly lost. The sensible, logical thing to do was to go on, down the trail to Wyoming and on into Colorado, if he failed to find Chip before then. Chip had come this way—at least he had crossed the Musselshell, and Billings was the first town south of there. Chip must have stocked up with grub somewhere, Weary told himself over and over. If he camped outside of town somewhere, of course the stablemen he had asked would know nothing about him.

Next morning he had a bright thought which told how close his friendship held him to Chip's affairs. He knew that Mike and Silver had been shod not so long ago, because Chip was fussy about his horses and hated to have their feet spread out of shape by running barefoot. And he knew too that Jeff was still wearing his old shoes. One thing and another had crowded in and Jeff's feet had been left—one of those odd jobs that are neglected until the last minute.

Before roundup started, Chip would have brought Jeff out of the pasture and shod him. Weary knew that.

And on the trail it was a cinch that Chip would hunt a blacksmith shop as soon as he hit town.

Weary had visited the one nearest the old Whoop-up Trail and was on his way to the next one when he saw a little man with a face like brown leather and a big hat and bowlegs and a gun hanging snug at his hip. Billy Burns, just coming out of the post office, shuffling a handful of letters and reading their addresses as he walked.

With one long step and a short jump, Weary was off the sidewalk and cutting across the street under the very noses of the leaders of a six-team freight outfit heading out of town. "Hi, Billy! Hold on a minute!"

Billy Burns whirled, stared, grinned widely and stuffed his mail into his coat pocket. "H'are yuh, Will? Kinda driftin' off your range, ain't yuh?" He went back a few steps, met Weary on the sidewalk edge and gripped his hand. "Heard you was ridin' north of the Missouri. You're lookin' fine. Kinda lengthened out a notch or two since I last seen yuh—or have I forgot?"

"Nope, you've shrank," Weary chuckled. "Have to look higher, that's all."

They swung into step, by common impulse headed for the nearest saloon, which at that hour should be quiet. Though it was early forenoon and neither man leaned to strong drink, they had a mug of beer apiece and faced each other, elbows on the bar.

"Well, what yuh been doin' with yourself, the last three-four years?"

"Ridin' for the Flyin' U—"

"Y'have? Know young feller about your size and

build—name of Chip Bennett?"

Weary set down his mug with a bang. All through the long length of him he stiffened. "Why? Anything happen to Chip?"

"Not a thing in the world—but there could of been plenty happen, if he wasn't just the kinda feller he is. Sharp as a steel trap, that boy. Friend of yourn, Weary?"

"Never thought more of a man in my life, Billy. I kinda hoped you could tell me where I can find him. That's what I'm down here for."

Billy Burns gave him a mildly speculative stare. "Wel-l, you just stick around a little and you'll likely see him. I'm looking for him to be siftin' in here with a bunch of stolen horses, most any time now."

"Mamma!" Weary ejaculated, after a startled breath. "If I thought you meant Chip had been stealin' horses, I sure would jam your works for yuh so you'd quit tickin'. You say Chip's due in here right soon?"

"Yeah, that's right. Way it started—come on over here and set down, an' I'll tell yuh about it." He led the way to a table in an empty corner, chose the chair with its back to the wall, and began shuffling a deck of cards that was on the table.

"Way the play come up, I was trailin' a bunch of stolen horses—no use goin' into the details of the case—and it led me over towards Crazy Mountains. Mebbe you don't know that country. You hit the mountains sudden, kinda like a wall, and there's one pass the road goes through.

"Well, they was about twenty-four hours ahead of

me, but I knew they'd hit for the pass. I found their camp—and also two dead men—deputies from Sweet Grass—hid in the brush. Way I figured it, they'd come up on these horse thieves where they cooked a meal and let their horses graze; in the night, the way I figured it out."

"Where'd Chip come in?" Weary's cigarette hung cold between his lips. His anxious gaze lifted from Billy's hands to his face, studying it, trying to read his thoughts ahead of the words.

"Chip Bennett," drawled Billy, "come in when I'd trailed my bunch over close to Bozeman and seen where four horses turned off and headed for town. That looked kinda funny, and I took in after 'em." He broke off to give Weary a keen look.

"Did this Bennett kid ever own a flax-maned mare and—"

"Two colts," Weary cut in. "Sure, he did. Brought 'em up from Colorado with him. Thought the world of 'em—talked to 'em like folks. Couple years ago he sold the mare and the oldest colt, he called Rummy—"

"That's the horse. That checks up to the last notch," Billy nodded. "That's one of the horses stole from a ranch outa town here about ten mile. Rummy. That's what he called the horse. Located him in a livery stable in Bozeman, along with another flax-mane that was a dead ringer for him—"

"Yeah, that'd be Silver. Year younger than Rummy." Weary leaned across the table. "Was Chip there in Bozeman?"

"That's what. There's where I cut his trail—cut it to

know who I'd been chasin'. I found 'im—"

"You ain't telling me Chip stole any horses. 'Cause if you do, I'll call yuh a liar and climb your carcass."

"Nope, I ain't tellin' yuh that, but I sure as hell thought it for a while. Went through his stuff that he'd left at the station—and say!" He slapped the deck down on the table. "That's what that picture was about! You! There was a tablet full of pictures somebody'd drawed of horses and different fellers ridin' 'em and gettin' bucked off. And there was one dandy picture of a feller turnin' hoolihans off'n a pinto horse, all tied in a knot. Looked awful familiar, but I was in a hurry and I didn't stop to figure it out. It was you."

"Mamma!" sighed Weary. "I thought I'd tore up that one. Chip musta made another one."

Billy waved it off as of no moment. "Yeah. Well, anyway, there wasn't a thing to tell who he was, so I arrested him in a roomin' house where he was poundin' his ear at noon—and that looked like a lot uh night-ridin' too. Took him to jail and started in on him."

"You—"

"No, hold on till I tell yuh. He told a straight story, about how he'd bought—or traded for 'im—that horse of Benson's. Claimed he sold the brown he had to a feller named Mosely, and it had got loose and come back into camp, and he was tryin' to find Mosely and return the horse.

"Well, he seemed like a pretty straight, clean boy—yuh get so you can spot a criminal, kinda, and he didn't have any of the earmarks. So I thought I'd just lock him up and see if I couldn't locate this Mosely and his two men, and the bunch of horses I'd been trailin'. And damned if I didn't wake up and find myself locked in a cell and this Chip feller gone. He'd wrote a note tellin' me he was gone to git Mosely—"

"When was this?"

Billy turned the question off with his fingers. "No matter—I took in after 'im quick as I got let out. They'd all headed off in the same direction, and I gave a guess and cut acrost and rode up on 'em just as your friend had glommed two of the bunch—one he called Mosely. It was Slick Robbins, about as mean and slippery a cuss as there is west of the Mississippi." He picked up the cards again. "I brought Slick and the other feller right on in. Slammed the door on 'em last night about midnight," he drawled, and began shuffling again as if his story was done.

"And where's Chip, then?"

"Chip," said Billy with a grin, "is having it made up to him for being called a horse thief and a murderer. Chip's bringin' in the third man and the horses. They'd run off a ways, and I give him a star and told him to go git 'em."

Weary pushed back his chair. *"Alone?"*

Billy absent-mindedly licked a thumb and, having finished what he had to say, started laying down the spread of a solitaire game. It was purely habit, however. Even while Weary was staring at him, waiting for his answer, Billy swept the cards together.

"I like that kid," he stated, with seeming irrelevance. "I like the way he sticks to a thing, and I like the way he handles a mean job. There's a girl over there—got herself into as mean a spot as you ever seen. Mary Allison. I've knowed her since she was just a little tad beggin' rides on my horse. She'd run her horse up the bluff onto a high shelf, thinkin' there was a goat trail on over the top. There wasn't. It had broke and slid off. This Chip friend of yourn—"

"Oh. Mixed himself up with another girl," interjected Weary, and relaxed again into his chair.

"Yeah. Them things happen awful sudden, sometimes. Well, he laid out Mosely and one of his pals. *Alive,* mind yuh! Any damn fool with a gun can shoot to kill, but he had 'em all hog-tied nice with their own saddle strings, and gagged so the girl Mary wouldn't hear their cussin'; foul-mouthed as hell. And then, this Chip feller goes up and gits Mary's horse down. About as slick as anything I ever seen."

"Well, and who's helpin' him bring—"

"Oh, yeah. I was going to tell yuh. Well, he'd got the best of me in that Bozeman jail, and busted off after Mosely by his high lonesome. And got 'im, by thunder. Then I rode up on him, and it was touch an' go there for a minute—whether he'd stampede or not. He's proud, and I like that in a man—when he's got anything to be proud about. I figured he did have."

"All wool and a yard wide," Weary murmured. "They don't make 'em any finer than Chip."

"Yeah. So these horses they'd stole, and some Mary was drivin' home to Laughin' Water—I used to work for Babe Allison, eight-ten years ago—they'd been drove off up the coulee outa sight, and the third feller

167

had sneaked off up there after 'em. I kinda wanted to show that young rooster I didn't harbor any grudge for that sock he give me there in jail, yuh see. And I wanted him to know I savvied he's straight as a string. So I deputized him and told him to go git that man and that bunch of horses, and take 'em over to Laughin' Water. Mary, she's stuck there on that ranch and wouldn't have another chance in ten year, maybe, to git acquainted with a good-looking feller like him, educated, draws pictures, writes a good hand—"

"Mamma!" gasped Weary, grinning in spite of himself. "You stopped your outlaw-getting to try and rib up a romance there?"

A peculiar smile twisted Billy Burns' lips. "Well, Mary's an awful nice girl, pretty as a picture. Will, if you was to see her once—"

"Hell!" snapped Weary, suddenly losing patience. "Did you send Chip *alone?*"

Billy Burns paused in the act of licking his thumb again. His eyes lifted to Weary's worried countenance in perfect guilelessness.

"Can't yuh see how much it meant to him—and to Mary—to give him that job and let him do it himself, without anybody else to take the credit? Sure, I sent him alone. What do you take me for?" And he added shrewdly. "Ain't he capable?"

Weary studied that. He sighed. "Oh, sure, he's capable. I s'pose you left him over there to visit awhile," he said sarcastically. "Seems funny to me you didn't wait and all come in together. What's the joker, Billy?"

The little man eyed him keenly. "The joker seems to be that you know Chip Bennett a damn sight better than I do, and yet I trust him a damn sight more than you do."

"That ain't so and you know it." Weary's voice was too gently expostulating to give offense. "Trouble is, it would mean a damn sight more to me than it would to you if anything happened to him."

"Nothing will. Lady Luck rides with that kid and don't you forget it."

"And trouble rides the wind. I don't feel right about it, somehow. It ain't my place to tell you your business, Billy, but seems like if you'd waited—"

"I waited till noon the next day," Billy told him, meaning reassurance. "Then I started out with my prisoners and left word for the kid to follow me." He swept up the cards and stood up. "He oughta be along most anytime now. Want to come on up to the court-house? I've got some letters to write—"

"No, don't believe I will. Some things I want to do."

At noon he hunted up Billy Burns again "Chip showed up yet?"

Billy Burns shook his head, studying Weary covertly. "I kinda looked for him before now," he confessed. "'Course, driving a bunch of horses—"

Unconsciously Weary hitched his gun forward. "If you'll tell me what road he'll come in on, I'll ride out and meet him," he said, in a tone of deliberate restraint.

"Sure it wouldn't make him mad, seein' you tryin' to ride herd on 'im?"

"Mamma! Let him get mad if he likes. I've got a present I promised to give him."

Billy Burns pinched out his cigarette, tossed it into the gutter and swung into step beside Weary. "Guess I might as well go along," he said mildly. "My horse needs exercise, anyway."

Under such thin excuses did they try to hide the uneasiness they felt, knowing all the while neither was fooled. They left the town and rode steadily westward until dusk. But they did not meet Chip Bennett.

CHAPTER TWENTY
"WHAT'S THE MATTER, MR. BENNETT?"

On the rocky tip of a high, barren pinnacle, Chip stood flat against a four-square boulder and stared down into the wild country he had just left. He saw eagles floating above a steep pine slope, two of them circling and looking as he looked, but with another interest than his. He saw the rusty gray-brown shape of a grizzly bear go shambling up over a stony ridge off to the right of him, two cubs at her heels making little scurrying side trips of their own, to be cuffed back into the trail by their huge mother.

For awhile he watched them, debating upon the chance he would have of a tender bear-cub steak, if he should drop down on the far side of the peak and meet them as they climbed up out of the deep ravine toward which they were heading. But grizzlies were bad medicine, especially an old she with cubs; and she might change her course and not cross the ravine at all. And anyway, it was a wild idea he would never carry out, because he didn't want to waken the echoes with a shot until the man he was after was lined up with his gun sights.

Moving slowly and keeping close to the rock, he circled the chimneylike peak and stood looking down to eastward. Wild country, that; seamed with canyons, broken where jagged pinnacles thrust up above deep, wooded basins. Practically impassable unless one knew the winding secret ways.

No country for horses, certainly. Yet down there somewhere a herd of more than thirty stolen horses had disappeared, Jeff and Silver among them. He tried to see just where it was he had lost their trail in a little rock-floored basin that had looked as if it might easily be turned into a natural corral. The horses had gone in there, he was sure of that much. Gone in and vanished.

Twice he had fought brush, climbed ridges, led Mike scrambling in and out of deep unsuspected gulches, circling that odd little basin, trying to cut the trail of those horses where they had gone out. The second circle had been wider, and darkness had come down and caught him unawares, he had been so hotly eager to pick up the tracks.

He never found the basin again; never found his back trail. With all his supplies packed on Jeff, and with the need of silence upon him, he fasted for two full days before he knocked a grouse out of a tree with a rock, as he had done once before. In a sheltered niche he built a small fire and broiled and ate half the juicy meat. Mike nibbled the small branches off some green shrub

171

Chip could not name. No use blundering around in the dark—they spent that night in the shelter of the rocks and were abroad again at dawn. Smoking was a luxury he could not afford; all his tobacco save a pinch or two was in the pack on Jeff—or had been—and he had to save his matches to cook whatever he might be lucky enough to get.

Another day. Another night. And now this day, when he had climbed this small sharp pinnacle to see what he might discover. Miles away, he could see the long and narrow valley he had left to follow the third outlaw and bring him back with the horses. It looked like a long strip of shimmery green silk pressed flat and smooth. Not so many miles, as one of those eagles would fly—more than two days of hard travel, as he had come.

To the north—he jerked his hat low over his eyebrows and squinted his eyes to see at a sharper focus. Minutes he stood rigid as the rock behind him, gently chewing a corner of his lip while he stared and studied, tried to guess ground distances; tried to fix certain peaks and ridges in his memory, as they would probably look from that rough country below; tried to map the most feasible route.

Yet it wasn't anything much that had caught his attention. A glint of blue, looking no bigger than a barrel top. A rim of green around it. A lake deep-set among precipitous slopes, bare rimrock walling it in. An age-old crater, filled with the soil made in the slow centuries by erosion, by rain and snow washing down particles of disintegrated rock—by all the mysterious alchemy of nature's laboratories.

And now grass was growing there in that deep, secret little valley; though it might not be so small, at that. It was only through one small notch in the surrounding cliffs that he could glimpse it at all. Except that it could not extend beyond that frowning rimrock or the jagged peaks to the north, there was no way of telling how large the basin was. It might fill all the space indicated by its impassable boundaries, or the inner rim might slope steeply down to a small center. From where he stood, he could only guess.

But it was there. With its enclosing barriers it could not be a part of the long valley; too far away, and the distance all on end. If he'd had glasses (those fine ones with his name stenciled on, that Weary would like to lay in his hands, for instance) he could have learned a great deal more about the place and perhaps found the easiest way to reach it.

But those glasses of which he had never heard were a long, long way from where he stood. His own keen eyes must serve as best they could. It had to be a gamble, anyway, though the chances would have been more in his favor if he had been able to see in greater detail.

For awhile longer he stood there, hungrier than he had ever been in his life before, studying the hills and ridges, the deep canyons he must cross. From where he stood, it looked pretty hopeless, but he meant to reach that little spot of blue and green in spite of everything. Somehow he felt that he would find there all he had been seeking. Maybe more; maybe a lot more than he was looking for, he told himself prophetically, and edged back around the rock to the place where he had climbed the peak.

Hours later, he was holding a stunned rabbit up by its heels, eyeing it hungrily and wondering whether he could stomach the meat raw and avoid the risk of making a fire, when suddenly there came to him an alien sound that set his back hair tingling.

He was down in one of the tortuous canyons he had seen from the pinnacle. He had found a spring seeping out from under a rock where the ground leveled off and the grass was thick and high, and he had loosened the cinch and slipped off the bridle and left Mike to graze on his picket rope. He had twice missed the rabbit, because his arm was shaky from lack of food, and had finally knocked it over with a lucky third throw. And while he stood there, he heard the clink of a horse's shoe striking a rock.

Instantly he dropped the rabbit and pulled his gun as he ran to shelter. The quick thumping of his heart angered him, made him fear he might miss, it seemed to shake his whole body so. But unless he was forced to do it, he would not shoot—he wanted to take the fellow alive and unhurt.

As he waited, he heard again that telltale, dull clink, closer this time. Mike heard it too and lifted his head for one brief glance and went back to his grazing, too hungry to care who was coming. A single rider, by the sounds, coming up the canyon rather slowly, though the way was fairly clear and easy to travel. But he was considerably heartened too. That rider seemed to prove that Chip had guessed right—that this was the way into that deep little valley. His luck wasn't running so dead against him, after all.

As the horse came on and could be vaguely glimpsed through the thin branches of a white-trunked aspen thicket, Chip moved stealthily closer to the point where he would have a clear view and yet be shielded by a rock heap, if it came to fighting. It was going to be a cinch. He'd have the drop right at the start.

Then Mike gave a half-hearted inquiring nicker, which killed completely the element of surprise. With an oath for the horse, Chip leaped out into full view, gun up,—and stopped where he was, heart standing still. Minutes it seemed that he stood there, frozen with astonishment, though in reality it was a scarcely noticeable pause.

"Are you in the habit of riding in the most dangerous places you can find, Miss Allison?" he asked, in what sounded like cold displeasure—putting it mildly.

She held in the black horse, staring at him wide-eyed. "You—you don't seem very pleased, Mr. Bennett," she countered, easing the reins a little to let Blackie go forward.

"Am I supposed to be pleased? You're in pretty wild territory, if you only knew it."

She glanced up at the frowning canyon walls. "I know it, all right. This is farther than I've ever been before."

Chip snorted, "I should hope so!" and slid his gun into its holster. "You came within an ace of getting shot, if anybody should ask you."

The brusqueness of his manner was a mask he used to hide the startled confusion he was fighting. That she should ride up on him now, after more than three days of fruitless searching, and find him still baffled, stung his pride. She must think him a regular false alarm. To let a man with only half an hour's start of him get clean away with a bunch of stolen horses, made him seem a pretty poor excuse for a range man. Or maybe she had decided that he was in cahoots with the thief. He couldn't blame her much if she did.

She slackened her reins and let her black horse crop a mouthful of grass while she looked at Chip.

"You've been gone so long," she said, "I just thought I'd better hunt you up and see what had happened. What's the matter, Mr. Bennett? Haven't you found the horses yet?"

CHAPTER TWENTY-ONE
MARY ALLISON

A futile, foolish anger seized Chip; anger because he was shaking as if he had ague. "Do you—see them around anywhere?" He reached out hastily to the rock beside him, clung to it for support. He wanted to lie down—wanted her to go away—

Mary Allison had been born within ten miles of where she now sat on her horse, looking down at Chip. She had seen a lot in the fifteen years she could remember. Death, mortal sickness, gunshot wounds— men staggering in to the ranch half dead from the hardships of the trail. She knew gaunt-eyed hunger as she saw it now.

She kicked off the slipper-stirrup from her left toe, slid her skirt-swathed right leg over the leap-horn, leaned sidewise, and slipped to the ground as lightly as a bird folds wings and settles upon a branch. She turned and untied a bulky roll of cloth from behind the flat cantle, tucked up her riding skirt somehow under her belt at the side, and came over where Chip stood watching her with set jaws.

"Let's eat," she said practically. "I'm starved. I left the ranch early, just as soon as papa and the boys were out of the way. I don't know how you're fixed for grub, but I do know you couldn't have had much when you left—unless you had a pack outfit back somewhere out of sight."

"I did have. He and another horse were annexed by our elusive horse thief on his way out."

"Well," said Mary, "I kind of suspected something of the sort. Anyway, I knew you wouldn't be making fires very often, unless you're greener than you looked. So I brought along some rations to see you through."

"Thanks. I was going to cook a rabbit—" He turned and looked at the place where he had dropped it. The rabbit was nowhere in sight.

Her glance had followed his. "First catch your hare—"

"I had him. Then you came along, making enough noise for a herd of buffalo—" He was talking at random, brutally, trying to keep his eyes off the flour-sack she was opening.

177

"Well, this is all cooked. Corn bread stays with a person better than white, so I brought johnnycake with lots of butter. And the roast beef is fine for the trail. Just help yourself, Mr. Bennett, and if you're as hungry as I am—"

Chip was, and proved it in the next few minutes. "What kind of jam is that?" he wanted to know, after his third piece of corn bread buttered and spread thick with a sweet, rich preserve.

"That? Plum and wild cherry mixed. Mamma made it. I wish I could have carried a jug; I'd have brought some fresh buttermilk. But it jounces around so if a person rides off a walk, and I didn't know what I might bump into. I didn't want to be bothered with any old jug if I got chased again."

Chip swallowed the last bite. "What did you come for? It wouldn't help matters any to have you cornered again." He had the grace to smile at the girl. "Poor time for me to raise a howl over your coming, though, and bringing something to eat. I admit it was welcome."

"Even if I'm not, I suppose." And she tossed her head in the way he remembered so clearly.

"I wasn't thinking that, exactly. But you must admit there are safer places in the world than these hills right now. You'd better go back, Miss Allison. And thanks for the johnnycake. It was a lifesaver, all right." And he added in the most friendly, human tone he had yet used, "I was about all in and that's a fact."

Her eyes dwelt upon him in friendly speculation. "You don't have to tell me that, Mr. Bennett. I knew. I wanted to come yesterday—before that, even. But papa and the boys were home, and I couldn't get away. When you didn't come right back that night with the horses, I just knew that fellow had given you the slip somehow. Billy Burns went on with his prisoners and left word for you to follow right along. But this is the third day, Mr. Bennett. It was time somebody came to see what was wrong."

With the last of his tobacco Chip was rolling the thinnest cigarette a man could smoke. Mary Allison watched him for a minute, then reached into a mysterious deep pocket and brought up a full sack of tobacco with wheat-straw papers attached. She tossed them to Chip as if it were the most natural thing in the world for a girl to do.

"I kind of thought you'd be out," she smiled. "I'm always following my brother around with matches and the makings. Men are so heedless about their own comfort." She added a small box of matches. "Now tell me what happened."

With a mental shrug of surrender, Chip nodded thanks, opened his cigarette and shook the tobacco into a fresh paper, adding to it from the full sack. As he caught the dangling drawstring between his white teeth to pull the sack mouth shut, his eyes met Mary Allison's. Both were a little breathless when the deep gaze broke of its own intensity, and Mary's cheeks were aflame. Chip hid behind his cupped hands seconds longer than it took to light his cigarette.

"Nothing happened," he said gruffly, harking back to the stolen horses as to a refuge. "I know there was a mule in the bunch, and I think now it was along because it knows the way to their hide-out and would go straight back there, and because horses will follow a mule where they wouldn't anything else but a bell." He was talking fast, wanting her to forget what his eyes had just told her before he realized their betrayal.

"You—they gave you the slip?"

"They certainly did. Horses can cover a lot of ground in half an hour or so, especially if they've got a leader and somebody behind to haze them along."

She was laying little pleats in her riding skirt where it fell smoothly over her knees. Though she did not meet his eyes again, her mouth curved in a smile. "There isn't much I don't know about driving horses. I've helped my oldest brother herd them ever since I could sit on a horse without falling off."

He bit his lip, held by an odd constraint from making some sarcastic retort. "Well, I tracked them till almost dark and lost the trail in a rock basin about the size of a good big corral. I couldn't find where they went out and I never did pick up the trail again."

"Then what are you staying up in here for?" Still she did not look up from her busy fingers.

For some moments Chip smoked in silence watching her slender brown fingers smooth and pleat and smooth again the dark cloth; watching too how her corn-yellow hair fell softly from under the old felt hat she wore today. Not so very long ago he had lost his handsome head over a girl with hair as yellow as that. Goldilocks, he had called her—and hated himself afterwards for his sentimentality. The thought of her came now unbidden and he frowned it away. She

180

wasn't to be remembered in the same day with Mary Allison, he told himself angrily. A girl like that—a double-crosser. Mary Allison's little finger was worth more than the whole of Julie Lang, for all her beauty.

"It seems to me," Mary said again, "you're just wasting your time. They could be clear over into Idaho by now. Probably they are."

Chip glanced up at the sun, glanced at Mike, made a quick estimate of the further time he could afford to give the horse.

"They can go to the Pacific Ocean and I'll be on their trail," he said, with a certain tenseness of purpose which betrayed his hidden hurt. "They—or he, if there's only the one man—got away with a horse of mine I think more of than any human on earth. I'll never stop hunting till I get Silver back, to say nothing of my pack horse and outfit. It isn't just the badge and being deputized, or even your horses—much as I want to get them back. I've got a crow of my own to pick with that—man."

"But if you lost his trail and can't find it again, what's the use of staying in these hills?" she urged.

"Because I think I know where they are. I was heading for the place when I came on this green spot and stopped to let my horse fill up." His glance strayed again to Mike, who was still hungrily biting off thick tufts of grass. "I've got to keep him in condition, no matter whether I eat or not. I'm liable to need all he's got to give, before I'm through."

Mary gave him a quick look, pulled the floursack close, ran one arm deep inside it. "You can't do much if you're half starved," she declared firmly. "That's why I brought along some trail rations; so if you're bound to stay out a few days more, you can eat. Here's pemmican. Ever taste it? The Indians make it and they trade it for jelly and jam and tea. It's good—if you're real hungry."

"I'll bet it is. But you shouldn't have bothered—"

"And here's jerky that mamma and I made. I guess you've chewed on that, lots of times, to stave off your appetite. It comes in pretty handy when you're caught out without grub."

"I'd tell a man!"

"Well, and here's a little sack of corn I parched while I was washing the dishes this morning. That's good to eat while you're riding along, too. I nearly always have some in my pocket."

"Miss Allison, I—"

"I'm not Miss Allison," she broke in upon his stumbling thanks. "I'm Mary to everybody in the valley. Even the Indians call me Mary. I don't like to be Missed all the time."

"Well, then, I'm Chip. I don't like being Mistered."

They laughed as if it were much funnier than it was, and in their laughter the constraint between them was forgotten.

"Well, now you're heeled, so far as food goes. But if you've found out where the horses are, and the thieves, I do think you should wait and have help. You can't do anything alone, you know."

"I don't know why not."

"I do, then. There'll be more than just that one man

there, you see. There's a regular nest of them some- where in these hills, only nobody has ever found out just where it is. The other day is the first time we've ever had any trouble—"

"Those fellows had been drinking all the way out from that little burg down the valley. I saw two bottles they'd thrown away. That might account for them tack- ling you."

"Very likely. There's a saloon in Spring Valley, the place you mean, and papa thinks the saloon keeper is friendly to the Thompson gang on the sly. But really, we haven't lost a horse even, until the other day. Nei- ther has anyone else in the valley—though there are only two outfits, for that matter; and papa thinks they're like the saloon keeper, friendly with Thompson. So really, nobody has ever really tried very hard to find where they hang out."

"Who's this Thompson?"

"Burt Thompson. He has a sort of ranch up north here. But he always has twice as many men hanging around there as he could possibly need, even in roundup time, and he doesn't seem to spend much time ranching."

"Is that the place I saw from the top of a pinnacle away back there—a place with rimrock around two sides at least, and a lake of some sort, maybe not very big, in a hay meadow?"

She gave him a prolonged, frowning look while he described it. "There's no such place as that in this whole country," she said, frankly puzzled. "You must have things mixed somehow in your mind. You're thinking of some other place."

"Oh. Am I?"

"You certainly must be. Burt Thompson's ranch—where the house is—sets in a grove just about at the top of a pass where the hills are lower, and it isn't more than six or seven miles from our valley over into Oxbow. We don't see much of him or his cronies. They go out the other way, as a rule; down Oxbow. I don't know why those men brought their stolen horses up our valley, unless they were drunk. Billy Burns thinks they were headed for Thompson's, all right."

"Then, why didn't he tell me about it? Why leave me to blunder around in the dark?"

She looked at him gravely. "He never dreamed it was going to take days and days," she said simply. "He thought the man would kind of hold the horses at the head of the coulee, waiting for the other two. He was sure you'd be back soon."

What Chip said to that was under his breath, as he got up and went over to Mike. He was slipping the bit into the horse's mouth when Mary spoke just behind him.

"You aren't going up to Thompson's, are you?"

"I'm going," Chip said, in his most deadly polite tone, "to go where I expect to find what I'm after."

"You'll find a lot more than you expect, if you aren't careful."

"I might."

"Well, if it's that rimrock valley, or whatever it is, I can help you."

Chip drew the cinch tight, tied the latigo with negligent ease and turned, looking down into her flushed, stubborn little face.

"You've done more now than you ought to have tackled," he said, worriedly gentle. "What you'd better do is go home and stay there. You shouldn't have come in the first place."

She opened her lips to remind him of the very substantial meal she had brought him, then closed them again without saying anything at all. In absolute silence she twisted and tied the top of the sack, gave it to him and watched him tie it behind his saddle.

He turned again to where she had stood, but she had gone to mount her own horse, so he stepped into the saddle and reined close, watching how lightly she went up, her long skirt seeming no hindrance at all. Funny, he thought, how women bundle themselves in cloth that would make a man helpless as a hobbled horse, and then tried to do a man's work on horseback. He was willing to bet it was Mary's mother made her wear that awful skirt. She'd have shown better sense if she'd kept her daughter home.

"I believe I know that rimrock you mean," she said. "I've been up pretty close to this lower end. But I certainly never knew there was any meadow or pond or anything of the sort down at the foot. Are there some jagged ridges, sort of a sawtooth line of hills, over to the west?"

"That's the place. I was up where I could look in through a gap and see the meadow."

She settled herself in the saddle, tucked her skirt down under the knee that rested over the leap-horn.

185

"Well, come on, then," she called briskly. "It's only about four miles from here, I imagine. But they're rough old miles, I can tell you. We'll have to go back down this canyon and take the next one over. I'm not absolutely sure, but I don't believe there's any way to get in from this side—"

"Now look here," Chip cried half angrily, "there's no way for you to get anywhere but back home. You must see—"

"I do see that you need a guide."

"Not on your life. Not you, Mary. I'll have my hands full enough without having you on my mind."

"You don't have to have me on your mind. Nobody asked you to."

"I don't know what I'm going up against. I can't be bothered taking care of you, and if you had any sense, you'd know that."

"Well, as it happens, I do know it. You don't have to take care of me, or think another word about it. Heavens and earth!" she exclaimed exasperatedly. "Do you think I came out here to be a drag on you? I can take care of myself, thank you. Look. I brought that gun you gave me of Slick Robbins."

"I don't care," said Chip, "if you brought a gatling gun. You're not going with me, and that settles it."

Mary thought it a long way from being settled, however. They quarreled bitterly about it all the way down the canyon. But in the end, Chip had his way. Mary started on home, tears of rage streaming unheeded down her cheeks.

When she was gone from sight, he still waited five

minutes just to make sure she did not try to trick him and follow along behind. There was no sight or sound of her. He reined Mike short around and started for the walled meadow.

CHAPTER TWENTY-TWO
GOOD-BY, MIKE

Courage and persistence will carry a man over obstacles that seem insurmountable. They carried Chip that afternoon into places any sane man would think twice about, before attempting them—and then would stop and think again. Chip thought as he rode, thought as he walked and led Mike, thought as he left the horse standing precariously among rocks fit to break his neck while he himself clambered over boulders and into some impassable gorge.

He spent himself to no purpose. By late afternoon he had pulled the heel off one boot, getting his foot free after a rock had rolled down against another and caught the foot as in a vise, he standing meanwhile like the Colossus of Rhodes, straddling a narrow crevasse in the hillside he was climbing. By good fortune and a long reach of his arm, he managed to retrieve the heel, and because the boots had been honestly made by hand, he was able to hammer the heel back in place with a rock and feel reasonably sure it would stay. But he did not climb that hill nor any other after that, confining himself to lower places, where a horse could travel.

By dusk he had given up hope. Actually he had turned back, knowing his quest to be an utter failure. He was going to find a place where Mike could find a little grass and rest that night, and in the morning he meant to call on Burt Thompson—as soon as he could locate the ranch—and get the truth out of him somehow. If that failed, he told himself glumly, he might just as well keep on going—or blow his fool brains out, and he didn't much care which. He certainly wouldn't face Mary Allison or Billy Burns or anyone else he knew; not after making this holy show of himself.

He was traveling downhill through a narrow rocky gorge he didn't remember—and didn't care whether he did or not. It led down to some other, larger canyon, and that was all that mattered anyway. One was the same as another. None of them were any damn good to him or got him anywhere. The girl was dead right, whether she knew it or not; he was just wasting his time.

So steeped in gloom was he that a hoofprint plainly marked in the sand between two flat rocks did not strike him as unusual or worth consideration. In fact, he thought it was Mike's track and let it go at that, not bothering to wonder how it was he had turned so complete a loop that he was now taking his own trail back.

It did strike him as peculiar, however, when he discovered that he was following some long-dried water channel and that he was facing a steep declivity that had once been a waterfall. Here the gorge was so narrow he could not turn back with Mike, and there was a lip of rock jutting out over a jump-off four or five feet to the slope below. Certainly he had never come up over that ledge with his horse. No one could.

In the half-darkness, he jumped off and left Mike standing there while he scouted ahead. It seemed a little lighter down below a way. Either he had come down one of the hundreds of tiny water courses into the wide canyon just below the one where he had lunched with Mary, or he had found the hidden meadow. He was sure it was the canyon, however; the meadow must be farther north. And he was also pretty certain now that he should have turned sharply to his right into a brushy gulch just after he saw the track. He had a vague recollection of coming into the gorge just about there, soon after he had left the canyon.

Too late now; too late and too dark to attempt going back. If Mike could negotiate that jump-off all right, the rest of the gorge looked fairly easy. But he was worried over that jump and he hated to have Mike try it. Still—

Perhaps he banked a little too heavily on his luck that had so far brought him through tight places safely. Or perhaps he had nothing whatever to do with it and the thing would have happened anyway. He was standing there below the drop, looking up and wondering how best it might be accomplished, when suddenly Mike took a hurried step ahead, thrust his nose down over the rock lip of the ledge, blew an impatient breath through his nostrils and took the jump.

"You, Mike!" cried Chip, too late to stop him. There was a rattle of rocks rolling together, the sound of hoofs scraping frantically for a foothold, the thud of impact as Mike fell, rolled half over and lay still, a dark, grotesque heap, with neither head nor feet showing but only the saddle riding the peak of the shadow, Chip's rifle thrust muzzle up to the thread of purpling sky where the handle of the Great Dipper showed over the rim of the gulch.

A broken neck; quick, merciful; grim reward of a horse's eagerness to be with his master. The suddenness of the tragedy stunned Chip, held him there dazed, staring. It wasn't possible, his incredulous mind kept thinking, over and over. Mike dead? Nothing doing! Mike was too sure of himself in rough ground. He'd tackled worse places than that and made it all right— you could trust old Mike to handle his feet anywhere.

Afterwards he tortured himself trying to remember whether he had called to the horse just before the jump, or just after. It hurt like the devil to think maybe he had called Mike to his death. He couldn't remember. Nor could he have told after it was over just how he had managed to get the saddle off without cutting the cinch. He did several things mechanically that evening, like a man walking and working in his sleep. To one who watched him, he would have seemed cool and calm and precise in all he did; in the way he shouldered the saddle finally and went carefully picking his way down the gorge, where black night had flowed in and he must grope his way through it like a blind man going down a strange corridor.

When he came out suddenly into starlit space and the fresh dewy smell of grass growing, he knew that he had found the secret meadow. But it did not seem to matter now so very much. With his thoughts all given to Mike and what his loss was going to mean, for the moment he forgot that it was here he had hoped to find Silver and Jeff and those other stolen horses.

He walked on with a dogged, apathetically plodding gait wholly unlike the Chip Bennett men knew, his shoulders bowed beneath an awkward forty pounds of saddle and the further weight of his rifle. More by instinct than intent, he kept to the edge of the meadow, just outside the line of brush and trees rustling in the night wind—a cowboy set afoot and packing his saddle into camp, by the look of him.

What he would do now he didn't know. As coherent thought came back, he saw that he must find those horses—stick to the job until he did find them. They might not be in this basin at all. It seemed too quiet, too empty. At that moment he had no idea of its size.

A lighted window blinking through the grove as he walked drew him as a light draws a moth. He watched until he saw it again through a gap in the trees, hitched the saddle into an easier position and turned off the grass into the grove.

The cabin, he saw as he drew near, was built of rock. He could not tell exactly, but it seemed to be of fair size; large enough, he judged, for three or four ordinary rooms. He was at one end, apparently, for there was a light farther down in another window. It was all conjecture on his part, because the treetops cast a deeper shade of darkness in the grove and he judged chiefly by the distance to that other light.

It might not be important—but a large cabin indicated more people occupying it at least part of the time. The very length of it bred caution. He swung the saddle quietly down to the ground, hooked his left hand around the horn and made his way up to the cabin corner. There he left the saddle, slid along to the window and looked in.

Voices had been coming to him in a mumble. He still could not hear all that was said, but he could see well enough. Four men sat at supper. At the end of the table, facing him, sat Mary Allison, with a cup of coffee in her two hands, staring at the four over its rim.

CHAPTER TWENTY-THREE
PRISONERS

Astonishment held Chip motionless. Could it be possible that he had wandered into Laughing Water Coulee at its upper end, and that this was the Allison house? He didn't see how that could be—and yet it was the only explanation of Mary's presence that he could think of. He stared, face pressed close to the window to see and hear the better.

The man at the end of the table nearest the window was talking, waving a fork to point his remarks. Across the flame of two candles Mary was looking at the man, her hair more golden than Chip had ever seen it, her eyes bluer. Her face, he thought, looked pale. As she listened, the red crept into her cheeks. She turned her gaze away from the man, lifted it—it seemed as though she must have seen Chip there looking in. His eyes seemed to meet hers for just an instant as her glance moved on, swung down again to the speaker.

"Pretty girl like you—" Chip heard, as the voice rose from a murmur. "—ideas in your head—settle down— know the difference—" And there was something about horses and good times, while the other three grinned and shoveled in their food.

"You wouldn't dare!" Mary interrupted the drone of that voice, her own tones clear and defiant, every word carrying distinctly to where Chip stood. "If you know when you're well off, Ed Hartman, you'll let me have our horses and go home before papa and the boys start out hunting me. As long as you left us alone, nobody bothered you up here. But when you stole our horses and—and brought me here, you upset your own apple-cart and you'd know it, if you had the sense of a rabbit."

So that was it! She'd been brought here a prisoner, even though she wasn't tied. No doubt they believed that she was absolutely helpless to do anything about it—that they were perfectly safe in giving her the freedom of the cabin while the four of them were there.

They simply did not know little Mary Allison. While they laughed at her—much as they would have laughed at a kitten humping its back at a pack of wolfhounds—Mary took a sip of coffee, her eyes like blue stars as she glared at the man she called Hartman. Then, like lightning, her two hands flung outward, dashing the contents of the cup straight across the table over the two candles.

Instantly the room was pitch-black. What sounded like Mary's box chair scraping and falling over, and the impact of something against the door, impinged upon Chip's consciousness as he left the window. Inside the room was uproar. Hartman was swearing, shouting, "Don't let her outa that door—!" And a man laughed loudly at the trick she had played. There was a confusion of tramplings, someone yelling advice—

Chip paid little heed to the noise. Already he was around the corner, leaping for the door with his saddle high above his head. Thoughts are swifter than light. His thoughts flashed straight to the truth—or what he believed was the truth. Mary had not rushed for the door, because she knew that was what they would expect her to do.

In the open space before the cabin, where the darkness was lighted faintly by the stars, he caught the dull reflection on the stone doorstep and halted just before he would have fallen. A black bulk appeared above it and Chip hurled the saddle. With a startled grunt the man went down, and what was no doubt a stirrup banded with iron snapped out and caught another full in the face as he lunged out on the heels of the first.

They sprawled, blocking the doorway. A third was too close, coming too fast. He stumbled over the heap and went headlong. Another, who must have been Ed Hartman simply because he had been farthest from the door, pulled up just in time, kicked and pushed his way out, wanting to know what the blinkety-blink they thought they were doing.

Him Chip knocked out neatly with the barrel of his

forty-five and turned and tackled the dim figure scrambling from the heap. A gun roared in a spurt of orange flame, and Chip felt the tug at his coat when the bullet went through. Automatically his finger squeezed the trigger of his own gun and someone screamed, *"Oh-h-h!"* the sound sliding down to a groan and a horrible moaning, with a queer bubbly gasping for breath.

"Get a light here, Mary!" Chip cried urgently. "My God, I can't shoot into this mix-up again—"

Against the stars an arm rose, gun gripped in desperate fingers. With his left hand Chip grabbed it, hung on, swaying, trying to see in the dark which body owned that arm.

He was too merciful. He could have emptied his gun into the heap and saved himself some trouble, but he was no killer. He would not shoot except in actual necessity. He was so made that he must give a man a chance—which sometimes seemed almost a pity. He located the head he wanted, leaned and struck.

Within the room a match flared, blazed and dimmed. "Oh, confound it, this wick is so wet—" Mary's voice, shrill with nervous haste. "Wait—wait a minute, Chip. I know where there's another candle—"

A minute more, her quick steps moving across the hard-packed dirt floor! Vague shadows as another match flame moved with her. Yellow light flaring and flickering, the shadows more clearly defined. Even as he stood there tense, on guard over the confused tangle of men's bodies, with the saddle somehow mixed up in the heap, the artist in Chip was subconsciously aware of the light falling aslant on the rough stone wall, the grotesque dance of the shadows.

Wide-eyed, Mary came with the candle held high, and stood in the doorway, staring down at the piled bodies. "Why, forever more! You certainly—" She stopped, gave a sudden hysterical laugh. " 'With the jawbone of an ass have I slain thousands and ten thousands,' " she giggled. "You look exactly like the fellow in the Bible." She caught her breath, shivered. "Are—are they—d-dead?"

"Not on your life." Chip's voice was quick, impatient—purposely harsh. "Hold that light lower, will you?" With a quick, absent movement, he pushed the gun back in its holster, caught the top man under the arms and heaved, straining backward.

"That's Ed Hartman," said Mary, with chattering teeth. "He seemed to be the ringleader, but I guess Thompson—Is he—?"

"He's gone bye-bye for a while, is all. I dragged my gun off the side of his head. There's one at the bottom of the pile I had to shoot. Have to get him out and see how bad off he is."

"I—I saw you peeking in—that's why I put out the lights. Ed Hartman and another one they call Poppy caught me and brought me here, but I—"

Chip was dragging Hartman inside, grunting at the dead weight. He seemed not to be listening, though the words registered automatically in one part of his mind while he planned.

"Set that candle on a box, will you, and rustle around and find some rope. I'd better tie these worthies up,

196

first thing I do. Can you find another candle?"

"There's a whole box of them over in the corner."

"Fine. Light all you can find something to stick them in. That jasper with a bullet in him doesn't sound so good."

So Mary, like an automaton lighted candles, a dozen or more, and stood them upright in their own melted grease which promptly congealed and held them firm on shelf and table. Three in whisky bottles she set on the box beside the door. She did it in snatches, interrupting herself to run with whatever rope she chanced upon, as the shadows fled from littered corners.

She helped Chip carry the wounded man in and lay him upon a bunk in the second room, and brought still more candles until the place was radiant with light. From without, the cabin looked as if a party were going full swing; inside, the activity was grim enough, with few words and no gaiety whatever.

"It's a lung," said Mary, wiping pink bubbles from the man's mouth.

"Nicked it, maybe. Too far over to go through the thick part. Smashed a shoulder, though."

She was steadier now. This was nothing she had not seen before. "You'll want bandages—and I don't suppose there's a sheet in the whole place."

"Oughta be flour sacks. Empty a bag if you can't find a clean one any other way. The flour won't hurt—it's good to stop the blood."

"I know—mamma saved a man that cut his foot with an axe and was bleeding to death. She just used flour—"

"Wait. Come and hold this compress down. That sack's too heavy for you. I'll empty it."

Thriftily Chip kicked a box over, open side up, and dumped the flour in that, simply because no sane man in the remote places will waste food deliberately, and he had too lately known the pinch of hunger; knew it now, for that matter. The crude surgery went on, was finished at last, Mary standing beside the bunk, holding a candle in either hand.

"Did you finish your supper?" Chip asked abruptly. "Let's eat."

"And leave these—?"

"What can they do?" he countered. "They can't hurt anything. We've got this situation hog-tied, little Mary."

She was still blushing when they sat down to a belated meal. But her eyes still held a worried look. Then, without preparation, it came out into speech.

"Did you notice, Chip, how Ed Hartman gave a snort and then grinned, when you said the situation was hog-tied? I wonder what tickled him."

Chip poised a bite of cold, rare-broiled steak on the end of his fork. "Maybe because I called you—"

Her yellow braids shook violently. "He wouldn't think that was funny, because he—he—well,—"

"He wanted you himself?"

"Well, he said he did. He said he'd get a preacher to marry us. He said he could catch one easy, down around Virginia City somewhere, and take him out to a camp where I'd be waiting. I—think he meant it too." Anger flashed. "The beast! I'd never marry him, the

198

longest day I lived. But—anyway, that wasn't why he laughed."

Chip chewed meditatively, took a swallow of cold black coffee well sweetened. "I wasn't paying much attention," he admitted. "What I had on my mind was, how I'm going to get that cripple out of here and get him clear back to Billings alive. He's the jasper I was sent after, all right. I knew him by the way his nose is ploughed up. Looks like he tangled with a wildcat not so long ago. I saw him away back in Crazy Mountain Pass—"

"He's the one that stole our horses the other day, I know that," frowned Mary. "They're all out in the meadow, over by the pond that you said was here—and I said it wasn't. There must be nearly a hundred head of horses in the bunch, and I expect they've all been stolen; every last one of them."

"Didn't happen to notice a high-stepping chestnut with a flax mane and tail, did you?"

"Why, no. Or—yes, I did, too. I was looking for ours, of course, and we weren't very close, but I did see a light-maned horse, I'm sure." Then she puckered her brows and returned to the thing that puzzled her. "But Chip, *why* did Ed Hartman give a snort and a grin like that?"

"Trying to do exactly what he did do—worry you," Chip replied promptly. "Bluff, that's all."

She looked doubtful. "I don't know. He saw me looking at him and pulled the grin off his face. I wish I knew for sure what he had in his mind."

"Just as well you don't, if you ask me. Nothing

they'd teach you in Sunday-school, I'll bet."

Mary tilted a gallon syrup can over her plate, watched the thin golden trickle for a few seconds, stopped it expertly by suddenly righting the can. With a knobby piece of bannock in her fingers, she looked at Chip soberly.

"Just the same, I don't like the way he looked when you said that," she persisted. "It sort of makes me feel creepy—as if he's got the joker up his sleeve."

"He's welcome to keep it there. I'm not dealing him any cards, as it happens." Deliberately he grinned at her. "Just to satisfy you, though, I'll go take a look around outside; see how many horses they've kept up, how many saddles—" he waved a careless hand as he got up. "If you ask me, I'll say I think those four in there just about complete the gang. I'll know for sure when I come back. Want the windows covered, Mary?"

Without waiting to hear whether she did or not, he dropped the deerskin already nailed across the top of the window where he had looked in. Evidently there were times when the gang wanted absolute privacy. And if ever it was needed, he told himself grimly, now was the time. But he laughed as he pressed the hide flat at the bottom so no crack of light showed.

"After seeing my unprepossessing countenance peering in at you, you're liable to get the jimjams while I'm gone, watching for some other freakish face to appear."

"I will not." But he thought she looked relieved, nevertheless.

With extreme casualness he strolled into the next room, found another deerskin blind provided, dropped it into place and walked over beside the bunk where Ed Hartman lay on his back, staring furiously at the pole ceiling.

"Who are you expecting tonight, Ed?" he asked quietly.

"The hell with you! I'll see yuh—"

Chip stopped that vile stream of abuse with an open hand slap across the mouth. "One more yip like that outa you and you can have front teeth for supper," he snapped, and turned to the wounded man. "Who is it you fellows are looking for? Burt Thompson?"

Art Poppy, which was the fellow's name, turned his head and looked at Chip with pain-haunted eyes. "Feed me my own teeth if you want to," he snarled weakly. "You won't get a damn thing outa me." And he coughed, groaned and turned his face to the wall.

In the middle of the disordered room Chip stood and looked about him. The other two outlaws were still dead to the world; Chip's little taps with that forty-five of his had not been gentle—he being a thorough young man always careful to make a good job of whatever he undertook to do. They were well tied, he was sure of that. Humanly speaking, there was nothing whatever in their plight to amuse Ed Hartman.

Seeing that individual watching him, he shrugged his indifference. "You'd talk, all right, and talk fast, if I really needed any information," he said, with a curl of his lip. "You couldn't tell me any news, anyway." And he went out and shut the door behind him.

Mary turned anxious eyes upon him and he answered their question cheerfully.

"If those jaspers are tickled over anything right now, they certainly have got a queer sense of humor," he declared. "You needn't worry a darned bit over them. Don't go near them while I'm gone; they might not be too particular in what they said. Just keep this outside door barred—"

"Oh. Do you suppose—"

"I don't suppose a darned thing. I'm just using common, horse sense, is all. They've got a door here it'd take a battering ram to break, and iron bars top and bottom. No use wasting all that, is there?"

"Not if you think there's any danger—"

"I don't think a thing like that. But I'm liable to be gone half an hour, maybe more. I want to get an idea of this whole place. If you lock up after me, you won't have a thing to worry about, Mary. Have you still got that gun? Oh—wait a minute."

He slipped outside, was gone half a minute perhaps, and reappeared with his rifle in his hand.

"There isn't one chance in a hundred, Mary,—but if anyone should come prowling around here, trying to get in, I wish you'd fire three shots out through the window with this. Will you do that?"

"Y-yes, if you'll show me how it works. But why do you say the window?" Mary stood looking at the gun as if she thought it might bite.

"Just a notion. The first shot will break the glass, and the sound will carry farther. I want to take a look at that bunch of horses, if it's light enough to see anything in the meadow. If I hear anything—"

"I wish you wouldn't go off so far." Though she tried to hold her voice steady, in spite of her it trembled noticeably. "You—you might get hurt, or—"

A new light shone in Chip's eyes at that unconscious betrayal; but all he said was, "Not on your life! You look after our prisoners and keep a stiff upper lip. I'll be back pronto."

CHAPTER TWENTY-FOUR
THE GANG'S ALL HERE

Once before Chip had called those identical words to Mary Allison and he still had to make good on them. He thought of it now and hoped he would be luckier. At the beginning, it seemed as though he was going to be, for in the stable he found her horse Blackie. A few gentle slaps, and friendly relations were reestablished, so that in the dark he could set his saddle on and lose no time.

To find the herd was no trouble at all. As Mary had told him, there were at least a hundred horses feeding alongside the pond a quarter of a mile from the house, and when he called to Silver, the three-year-old came galloping toward him, coming from the far side of the bunch. More slowly Jeff came ambling up to his master, and for the time being, there was no more to be accomplished there.

With his own saddle on Silver and the empty pack saddle on Jeff, he found Mary's sidesaddle by the light of a match or two, saddled Blackie, and led the horses some distance beyond the cabin, tying them in the grove. He hoped the precaution would not be necessary, but he would feel better knowing that he had not left everything to chance.

As he walked back to the cabin, he heard the hoof-beats of several horses galloping and stopped to listen. The sound came from farther up the basin; a bunch of the loose horses taking a run, probably, as young horses often do for pure pleasure in the chase. Nothing to worry about. They weren't coming his way, and he dismissed the matter from his mind and went on to the house.

"Mary?" He waited a minute, then knocked and called again. With his ear to the stout planks, he heard the inner door shut, and in a moment the girl called to him, was reassured by his voice and let him in. She was white and her eyes were big with fear. She leaned against the wall as if she needed its support, and when he spoke to her, letting the iron bars fall into their sockets, she only shook her head in answer, watching him bar the door.

Chip was no ladies' man. He was shy of women and he hid his shyness behind a certain brusque manner he had found useful before now. He took Mary Allison by both shoulders, backed her to a crude bench and sat her down none too gently, his young face stern as any parent.

"For the Lordsake, brace up!" he said roughly. "If you're thinking about fainting, I'll tell you right now that all I know to do for that is to douse a dipper of cold water in your face. You're all right. Safe as God's pocket."

He gave her a little shake and let go of her shoulders, and Mary gasped and looked up at him reproachfully, tears filling her eyes, spilling out over her cheeks.

Chip drew a long breath and tried again. "Well, what you want to cry for? Soon as it's daylight, we'll drift out of here. I've got our horses all saddled and ready, over here in the thicket. If that isn't good enough for you—" He lifted his shoulders. "What's the matter, anyway? You had nerve enough, a little while ago—"

Mary swallowed, fighting for control. "It's that man, Ed Hartman," she said, turning her eyes involuntarily toward the other room.

"What's the matter with him? He's not loose, and I'll bet money on it." Chip glanced over his shoulder and back to Mary.

"No, he's not loose, but—but he just lies there and—and *gloats!*"

"Gloats?" Chip frowned a little over the word. "What's he got to gloat over?"

"That's just it," Mary whispered hurriedly. "You wouldn't think he'd feel much like laughing, but he's in there now, grinning as if—well, as if he's tickled over some joke."

"Ah, forget it, Mary. He's probably tickled to think he's got you buffaloed."

"It isn't that. I know it isn't. He knows something. He looks as if we had just walked into a trap or some-thing. Somebody's coming, as sure as you live. He wouldn't have that twinkle in his eyes unless he knew

205

he'd be free in a little bit and we'd be the prisoners. Oh, Chip, let's go now, before they come! Never mind taking them back with us—you can't. Our lives are worth more than horses—"

Hands on her slim, brown wrists, he stopped her terrified pleading. His eyes, looking deep into hers, sent some vital message of cheer, of courage. His mouth stirred faintly, as if words pressed close behind his lips, were held there by his inflexible will.

"I know I'm acting like a fool," she whispered, half whimpering. "But all the same, I know somebody's coming. A bunch of outlaws—"

"Well," he grinned steadyingly, "let them come. They can't get in—they took mighty good care of that. Look at that door. Planks just about bullet proof, and those iron bars to make it stronger. Look at the walls, Mary. Rocks cemented together, a good two feet thick. And the roof is logs buried under dirt. It would hold up a herd of cattle, darned near."

"I know, but all the same I feel it in my bones we're just like rats in a trap, somehow. And Ed Hartman knows it and is lying in there laughing at us right this minute."

"Well, if we're trapped, so are he and his cronies. Look, Mary. I can put that plank shutter over the window." He lifted the heavy square of planks cleated together, showed her the narrow slits at each side, just large enough to slip a gun barrel through and sight along it. "See how a fellow can stand behind two feet of rock and take a shot at whoever's outside? They sure didn't overlook any bets."

"I don't care. There's something tricky about this place and I know it." Stubbornness braced her now. Chip had a fleeting thought that she was half hoping someone would come, just because it would prove her fears were justified.

She stood up, little and slim beside him, her golden head tilted back so she could look up at him. "You'd better go in and see for yourself," she said, keeping her voice low. "Take a good look at Ed Hartman when he doesn't know you're watching him. That's all. You just see the expression on his face and draw your own conclusions."

"I certainly will. And how about the rest of the bunch?"

"The skinny one was coming to, but he wasn't saying anything. The other one you must have hit an awful crack; he's still dead to the world, or he was. And the man you shot wanted water—that's why I went in there."

"Well, you can keep away from there now," Chip grinned, and walked over and looked into the water buckets. Both were half empty. His instinct was to take one bucket out and fill it, and his glance, sliding along the back wall, saw that it was perfectly blank, solid rock. Funny they'd have only one door in the whole cabin, and that set squarely in front. He looked at it, looked at Mary, and decided to leave those bars right where they were. One bucket of water ought to see them through until daylight.

With a cup of water he went into the other room which was filled with bunks; double deckers, twelve bunks in all; enough to hold twenty-four men if they slept two in a bed, he made swift estimation. And there was room on the floor for several more to spread their blankets, leaving the outer room clear of sleepers.

But it was queer, just the same, that this room had no outside door and only the one window at the end. There were places in the wall where coats, mackinaws, shirts—odds and ends of clothing—were hung on pegs set into the wall when it was built; set too evenly to satisfy Chip. With a casual sweep of his arm, he brushed aside an old coat of buffalo hide and saw the thing he had suspected was there—a loophole flaring inward like a funnel, slitted at the outer edge. The place was built for siege, no doubt about that.

Setting the cup on a rough table in the center of the room, he found a shutter for the high window, lifted the hide curtain and fixed the shutter in place. No reason in particular for that, but he thought he might as well be consistent and close this window as he had the one in the other room. That done, the cabin was like a fort. Mary needn't be afraid of anything less than a cannon.

"What you scared of?" Ed Hartman leered from the bunk where he lay.

"Not a thing in the world. Just don't want the night air blowing in on you gentlemen. Your health's damn delicate; don't yuh know that?"

Beneath his steady stare, the outlaw's eyes flickered, turned away toward an empty bunk against the back wall. And while Chip watched him, a furtive look of satisfaction grew in Ed's face; a look impossible to define yet unmistakably there. Mary was right, after

208

all. Ed Hartman was secretly gloating over something he feared might reveal itself in his eyes.

With a muttered oath, Chip strode across the room, rolled the man over and examined his bonds. They looked secure—they *were* secure. Chip would stake his life on those knots. Unless the rope had been cut— Just to make sure, he went over it inch by inch. It was nearly new, well stretched, strong enough to hold the biggest critter on the range. If Ed Hartman had any idea of getting loose, he must expect to perform a miracle.

But just to be doubly sure, Chip took an extra half hitch around the ankles, brought up the rope end and tied it to Hartman's wrists. He searched for knives, sent probing fingers looking for some cunningly hidden gun,—a derringer, for instance. He found a dagger in Hartman's boot, and that was all. So he tied him to his bunk with an odd piece of rope and left him to grin over his obscure joke.

He gave Poppy a Dover's powder which he found on a shelf, let him drink his fill, searched him very thoroughly and tied him in case a little of his helplessness was faked. The other two he served as he had Hartman, tying each man to his bunk. There did not seem to be anything else that he could do, unless he killed the four of them outright. And yet that sardonic laughter still lurked in Ed Hartman's eyes. Whatever it was, his secret joke was still unspoiled.

Chip searched the big room, found a lot of ammunition, a couple of knives, four rifles. He carried them out and dumped them on the floor in a corner of the living room, Mary watching him big-eyed.

"Well, what do you think now?" Her words were a challenge.

"Think? Oh, about Hartman? I think he'll be laughing out of the other corner of his mouth pretty quick."

"You admit he *is* laughing."

"If he is," Chip parried gruffly, "he's crazy; that's all I can say." His eyes were fixed upon a familiar-looking heap of blankets dumped carelessly in the corner along with some other things he recognized. "Look here, Mary," he called suddenly. "Here's my outfit. I guess that's proof enough we've got the man I've been looking for—"

He straightened abruptly, listening. Voices, footsteps were approaching, coming from the direction of the stable; muffled by the thick walls, it is true, but distinct enough for all that. With a hasty glance at the girl, he stepped close to the door and stood there waiting, his hand on his gun.

The latch rattled, hinges creaked as strain was brought upon them. "Open up there! Hell, what's the matter with you boys? Y' all asleep?" A pause, another rattle and a push. "Ed! Come alive!"

"It's the rest of the gang!" Mary whispered, standing tense beside Chip.

"Sh-sh. We'll keep them guessing," he whispered back, shaking his head at her.

With his ear against the plank door, he could hear the mutter of several voices as the newcomers discussed among themselves the possible reasons for the silence and the locked cabin—locked from within, at that—so early in the evening.

"Ed! Art Poppy!" and then, "Oh, Bill!" And they waited, puzzled and evidently beginning to be alarmed. One swore, and Chip glanced quickly at the girl, wishing she would go away and not stand there listening to everything.

Then suddenly someone in the next room yelled two short sentences that sounded Indian, though Chip could not understand the words. Outside, a voice yelled two words in reply.

"Ed Hartman!" gasped Mary, clutching Chip's free arm. "He's talking Blackfoot to them!"

"Know what he said?"

She shook her head worriedly. "I only got a little of it. One word meant *captive*, and then he said something—it doesn't make sense, but I thought he said something about a den. Fox hole, I think it was."

"And the one outside said all right, or good. Wasn't that it?"

"Yes, good. It means all right. What do you suppose—" She broke off the question as if she already knew the answer. "Well, the gang's all here, I guess," she said calmly, in the tone of one who has seen the end and is resolved to face it. She lifted the gun Chip had given her, looked at it grimly. "We're in for it, all right. Where's some more bullets when these are gone?"

Chip looked at the gun, stepped over to the confiscated guns and ammunition, chose a couple of boxes and tore them open, dumping the contents on the table.

"Same caliber as mine," he said. "But you needn't fight, Mary. Just watch that window and bang away if anyone tries to break in. You—do you still think you'd like to faint?"

"Oh, shut up!" she retorted, with a bleak little smile. "I'm only scared when there's nothing else to do."

"You're a brick, Mary." And he gave her a kiss and a pat on the shoulder before he went to stand beside the door.

CHAPTER TWENTY-FIVE
AN OLD SCORE TO SETTLE

An ominous silence had fallen outside the door. Listening intently, Chip thought he heard men walking back along the side of the house, and he got the impression that they were trying to be stealthy. At least, they were not talking, he was sure of that.

"Fox hole" might mean that small window at the farther end. He whispered to Mary, slipped across and into the bunk room. A whispering stopped instantly as he pulled open the door. Four pairs of eyes swung startled glances toward him. He went up to Ed Hartman, stood looking down at him until the bold eyes flickered, refusing to meet his steadfast gaze. He turned suddenly and caught a swift exchange of glances between the other two, broken guiltily the moment they felt themselves observed. Art Poppy watched him feverishly. No one spoke a word.

No use asking what they had on their minds. He

turned away, examined the window again, set the candles so their light illuminated the shutter. It was very quiet now outside. Too quiet. Too quiet within that room where four men lay bound with ropes until they could scarcely move a finger, watching him as trapped wild animals watched; yet different, too, for these watched with wise eyes that held some secret knowledge.

It gave him the creeps. Warning prickles of his scalp tried to tell him of danger. And yet, what chance was there in that room? He thought of some secret entrance, looked for it as he stood leaning in the doorway and rolled and lighted a cigarette. The rough stone walls, the rocks set in mortar, were solid—no chance there for a secret door. He looked for it, unobtrusively studying the way the rocks were set. No break anywhere in the construction save where the partition of eight-inch logs divided the cabin into its two square rooms.

The floor was of hard-packed dirt, the walls evidently built up from a trench all around as a protection from small animals. With swift glances he scrutinized the roof. There again the logs were fully eight inches thick, extending unbroken from ridgepole to wall. They lay so close together that some were hewn for a tighter fitting. No chance there, without a good deal of labor. No chance anywhere, so far as he could see. Strong as a prison or a fort, he would call it.

With a shrug of his shoulders, he dismissed the feeling that something inimical to himself and Mary lurked within that room. Evil enough, yes. But he had the fangs pulled, all right. Let them look.

Something banged against the outer door. Outside the kitchen window a rifle roared, and a bullet pinged against the rock fireplace and thudded into the log partition. Chip jumped for Mary, pulled her against the wall beneath the window, whispered to her fiercely to stay there and keep quiet. Another shot came through at a slightly different angle and buried itself in a log.

Beside the door Chip waited, one eye on the window, another on the door, his thoughts clinging mostly to Mary. Until he saw that they were likely to break through shutter or door, he did not intend to waste any shots. No use filling the place with powder smoke, he thought, unless he saw a fair chance of hitting someone. Let them blaze away.

For several minutes a desultory firing continued, and a vague uneasiness formed in Chip's mind. One gun was all he could hear. What were the rest doing, then? They were not battering against the door, and the farther window seemed completely overlooked—

His thoughts drew his eyes that way, through the open doorway. He stiffened, stared, left the door and darted to the inner wall, running on his toes as the heavy planks behind him jarred to the impact of a good-sized rock.

While Mary watched him fearfully, he stood poised beside the doorway, gun raised high, waiting for that sliding shadow he had seen on the bunkroom floor to move on and bring into view the man who was thus unwittingly betraying himself.

Once Chip moved his head. That was when he tilted

it backward, signaling Mary to slip along the end wall out of line with the doorway. From the tail of his eye he saw that she obeyed him and he nodded with a slight smile that did not leave his face, but hardened and gave him a look of deadly purpose, waiting there like a panther on a limb ready to spring upon its victim.

The man was cautious. His shadow halted on the very threshold. All Chip could see was the dark oval cast by a hatbrim, immovable on the hard earth floor. For an interminable pause it remained there, and he took the risk of another glance at Mary, his eyes imploring her to speak or move—do anything to break that impasse of utter silence.

Mary understood. She began to whisper so low that even Chip's keen ears could not catch the words, though it pleased him to see that she was making the faint sibilant sounds seem argumentative, as if two were in that far corner whispering and not agreeing any too well.

Then her voice rose in a real stage whisper: "No! Keep away from the door! Look out here, through this loophole. They'll never think of you being away over in this corner—All right—" in a deeper whisper, and then—"Can you see anyone?"

It was a remarkably effective bit of strategy. A blind man listening would have sworn that Chip was over there in the corner of the big room with Mary, face to the wall, peering out through a loophole.

The man behind the shadow believed it, for on the floor the small tip of an oval resolved itself into the outline of a high-crowned hat with a head inside it.

Shoulders took shape. Chip looked no longer at the floor but watched the doorway even with his face and lifted himself upon his toes, muscles tensed, ready to release that stance with the snap of coiled springs.

The blued barrel of a six-gun first appeared, the man himself close behind it. As his eyes sought the expected figure standing back to him against the far wall, Chip set his jaw and struck.

And in that instance he knew that he was felling Pete Riser, and the knowledge instantaneously flashed a complete picture against the fog of his surmises. Pete Riser the outlaw, member of Burt Thompson's gang. Thompson and Dunk Whittaker, the suave banker of Helena, sounded like smart teamwork somewhere—

That much, while Pete lurched forward and sagged his sprawling length within the room, his gun going off as he fell. As his body thudded upon the floor, Chip with his boot toe swept Pete's long legs aside and slammed the door shut, heaving his body against it.

"That bar over there—bring it here, quick!" he whispered.

Mary seized it and darted with it, laid it in the sockets made for it and sprang aside as a body pushed hard against the door. Sockets for two more bars. Whoever had built that rock house certainly left nothing to luck. The two bars dropped into place as fast as Mary could find and bring them, and Chip pulled her away with him as he stepped back.

"Pete! What the hell—" It was Ed Hartman's voice and he was thumping on the door and swearing viciously. "Damn you, Pete, if you touch that girl—"

While he threatened and pushed, Chip held Mary tighter. "Scream a little—not too much," he directed cautiously.

Which she did, adding a breathless protest or two for good measure.

"Pete! I'd laid out to marry that girl! You damn fool, open this door!"

"Aw, keep your shirt on!" Chip answered, trying to imitate Pete Riser's whining voice.

It didn't work. Someone in that room knew Pete Riser too well to be fooled.

"Lemme at that door," a new voice snarled. "They're playin' you for a sucker, Ed. I knowed it all along."

A six-shooter bellowed and a shot came through the door. Another. With a sweep of his arm Chip forced Mary down upon the floor, piled bags of flour around her. Within that makeshift barricade, she was a little safer from glancing bullets; left him free to fight.

The door, he saw, would give way under a determined attack, so he took measures to prevent one. The last comers—part of them at least—were ramming something heavy against the outer door, and shots were coming through both. But little Mary Allison behind her bags of flour began to shoot deliberately at the front door, her cheeks flushed with excitement and her eyes like blue stars. Someone out there yelped.

It was not from any reluctance to hurt that Chip held back his fire. He wanted those in the bunkroom to grow bold. With Pete's gun in his left hand, his own in his right, he set himself to emulate the two-gun men of legendary fame all up and down the frontier.

Until he heard the gruntings and saw the door shake under a massed attack he waited, then fired close and straight through the planks, using both guns. Again and again, and knew he had scored hits. Then at the window he peered through a slit and aimed at a man standing just a few feet away, loading his gun by starlight.

That man dropped. Another ducked out from behind the corner to drag him back—and fell across the first. And while Chip watched, no others appeared.

Standing where he was, he reloaded both guns, all but emptied them into the bunkroom, laying a pattern of bullet holes in the rough hand-sawn planks.

Mary ran out of ammunition, gathered up her riding skirt above her slim ankles, stepped over the wall of bags, dashed to the table and soon had almost all the cartridges there scooped into a fold of her skirt. She made a swift, safe dash back, leaped lightly into her nest, settled herself and reloaded the gun, to resume her grim battle.

Too late to stop her, then watching with his heart in his mouth until she was back where she belonged, a convulsive chuckle escaped Chip. That girl faint? Not on your life! Not until it was all over, anyway. Fight like a wildcat now and cry afterwards, probably.

Something rattled down the chimney then and pulled his attention away from the girl. Something black, with a dull gloss like coarse, waterworn black gravel (if gravel were ever black as that). Still firing methodically, standing against the partition now and reaching out a long arm to take aim close to the planks, he watched that slow, stealthy dribble, puzzled creases between his eyebrows.

Powder, that was it. Black powder. And he ran to the fireplace, thrust his arm up the wide chimney and emptied his six-shooter in a quick staccato of shots, spraying the bullets on all sides as he fired. The dribble of coarse powder ceased abruptly and something bumped the ground outside.

With a few hurried scrapes of his foot Chip cleared out the ashes, luckily cold. A dishpan half full of dirty water sat on a box near by. He set it in the fireplace instead, answered Mary's approving nod with a grin, and went back to his job; which was to make that bunkroom too warm for comfort and to discourage any further attempt upon the window.

Outside the fusillade slowed, stopped for awhile. The candles burned down to stubs; two guttered and flared in their pool of melted tallow, drowned themselves and went out. Chip laid Pete's empty gun on the table and went to get more candles, since plenty of light seemed to make their plight a little less grim.

He was stooping over the box when Mary cried out suddenly, a startled warning. Simultaneously there came a scuffling rush behind him. He whirled and ducked, catching the force of Pete Riser's onslaught on one shoulder.

Like fighting cats the two rolled and clawed at each other on the floor. Chip's hold on his gun was loosened as he went down, and with a snap of his wrist he managed to send it skittering across the floor as it left his hand. And after that it was slug and wallow, heave and strain and roll.

Since Pete went down inside the room, Chip had been walking around him, stepping over him, keeping a wary eye on him through the acrid haze of gunsmoke. He had used all the rope they could find in the cabin when he tied Ed Hartman and his fellows, and there had been no time to hunt anything else or to cut strings from one of the hides scattered about. So he had just let Pete lie where he had fallen, not even taking time to drag him off to one side out of the way. As a matter of fact, he had a vague idea that it would be better to leave him there in the middle of the floor in plain sight, where any movement would be noticed instantly.

No use blaming himself now. Pete had played 'possum, that was plain; but he certainly must have a mighty hard skull, Chip thought pantingly, to come out from under the wallop he had received. And Chip remembered too how not so long ago he had left Pete lying almost like a dead man—and had found him very much alive and on the job soon after. And there at the depot in Dry Lake he would have sworn Pete would stay down for an hour at least; but he hadn't; he had boarded the train he had meant to catch. Damn the coconut-headed sneak, anyway!

Chip always did have the faculty of racing his thoughts through and around and over any tight spot, and the tighter the spot, the faster they seemed to fly. Now he was remembering every trick and every hold that Pete Riser had used or tried to use down there in the Badlands, and he was using them first whenever he got the chance, and slipping in a few of his own.

Any faint hope that Pete was groggy from that crack on the head went glimmering. Pete was very much all there and he was fighting to pay off old scores besides making new ones. Chip had knocked him out of a nice bunch of money when he spoiled that little deal of Dunk's. Let him alone and he would jam things for fair, here in the basin. It is doubtful if he gave Mary Allison a thought, however—

Because if he had, he would have kept his weather eye on Mary. He fought cannily for one purpose—to reach the knife sheathed just out of sight in his boot. Let him get that in his hand and he would not ask odds of anybody.

Some vague suspicion of that knife made Chip wary. Always he managed to force Pete's hand up away from his leg, managed to keep him busy protecting his throat, grabbing at the long clutching fingers that threatened his eyes—though Chip had never gouged a man in his life and never would.

So for a time the fight was give and take, neither getting the better of it. But those last three days bad taken a heavy toll of Chip. While Pete Riser had filled his stomach pretty regularly every day, Chip had fasted. And he began to tire. His holds slipped and loosened too soon. Strain as he would, he could no longer throw Pete off him, get him on his back.

Chip did not know it, but Pete's head was spinning like a top. He kept shaking it, closing his eyes for a minute to stop the buzzing. He broke a hold, reached down just a shade too fumbling for his knife, groped for a second, apparently in some doubt as to whose leg he had touched.

His fingers touched the knife hilt, gripped and pulled it out, but awkwardly. He had Chip down, all right, just about where he wanted him, knee planted agonizingly in his groin, left arm pressed across throat and chest, hand clenched around Chip's wrist. He lifted the knife, shook that film of dizziness out of his eyes, peered to see just where to strike and be sure of the heart, then slashed savagely down where he thought the heart was.

And at that moment two things happened, and both were unexpected. Chip gave a convulsive heave, tearing his head away from that crushing arm, throwing Pete sidewise as he lifted himself up. And little Mary Allison, with Chip's carbine in her two hands like a club, swooped it around with all her might and—while she cracked Pete's jaw in passing and laid him limp on his back—could not stop there. The heavy gun barrel was carried on by its own momentum and sideswiped Chip on the top of his head as he was falling.

CHAPTER TWENTY-SIX
TRUST A WOMAN'S WIT

Perfectly horrified, Mary stood staring down at what she had done, or thought she had done. Then she saw the knife all wet and red where it had slipped from Pete's hand to lie against Chip's thigh. She dropped the gun and picked up the knife, shivered and cast it from her as if it were a snake.

"I ought to cut your throat with it!" she gritted, loathing eyes on Pete.

She knelt, saw where the blood was seeping out through Chip's shirt. It wasn't his heart, at any rate. Bad enough—terribly bad; but it wasn't a fatal thrust. At least, not immediately fatal. And there was something she had to do first.

She found a piece of strong twine and tied Pete's hands behind him, working fast to get it over with before he had time to get his senses back; throwing her half hitches as expertly as any cowboy and drawing them mercilessly tight. With the end of string remaining, she took a turn around his grimy neck in such a way that he would certainly strangle himself the moment he began struggling to free his hands.

There was no pity in her eyes while she worked over him, nor any in her heart. She had never been tied, herself, and perhaps she did not realize how painful a cord cutting into the flesh can be; or she wanted him to suffer for his sins. Whatever her reason for it, she made a very good job of binding Pete. He would not be comfortable, that was certain.

She did another thing that was purely feminine. Pete was beginning to blink, and he looked at her with a bewildered glassy stare when his eyes finally opened. So she pulled off his dirty neckerchief as if she were touching something foul—which she was, in a measure—and tied it with vicious yanks around his head, completely blindfolding him. Then she pushed him out of her way, spurning him with her foot, and went to work on Chip.

No flour-sack bandage for him. Instead, she tore up one of her three petticoats, which was white muslin trimmed with thread lace she herself had crocheted. Keeping out of the line of occasional bullets, as she moved here and there, she found a carbolic salve such as her mother kept on hand for wounds, pulled Chip's blood-sodden shirts up under his arms and proceeded very efficiently to close the three-inch cut gaping in a grisly red grin under his left breast, salve the wound generously on the outside and bind it as tightly as she could draw the cloth.

She tried to do exactly as her mother would have done, and she was so engrossed with the mechanics of the job that she completely forgot to feel any embarrassment, which was perhaps the final test of her intelligence.

She had Chip's head in her lap and was sopping a wet cloth upon the purpling lump where she had skinned the top of his forehead when he opened his eyes and looked up at her. One hand went groping up and caught her fingers, wet cloth and all.

"What happened? Pete knock me out?"

"Hush. No—I did. You got in the way."

He frowned, trying to collect his thoughts. "Then—"

"Don't worry about *him*. He's tied up tight and I just now stuck a potato in his mouth to stop his swearing."

"The deuce you did!" Chip grinned wryly, pushed her hand away—but gently—and started to get up.

Mary held him back. "No, keep still. That—*hell hound*—stabbed you in the side. It's quite a gash. I don't want you to start it bleeding again. I've got you all bound up, but you mustn't move around."

Chip considered that, biting his lip. "Well, if you could prop me up somehow—my bedroll over there, if you can drag it over to me. How long has it been?"

"Not so long. Half an hour, maybe; maybe more. There hasn't been much shooting. Some, but no more than there was. I fired a few times, just to show them we're still in the ring. I don't know what they're up to now. Nobody has shot for at least five minutes." She helped him up against his piled blankets.

"Then look out. They're cooking up something. Bring my gun, will you? The rifle too. Put a few rifle bullets through those planks and they'll have more power than a six-gun." He thought for a minute. "Bring all the guns and all the ammunition over to this corner, will you?"

She looked at him strangely, doubtful of his lucidity. But she brought the guns and all the cartridges she could find.

"There ought to be three or four boxes in my stuff over there. Look in the bottom of the kyacks."

She did so, found the boxes and brought them to him.

"What do you want them for? Why—"

"Just in case. Could you drag those flour sacks over here, Mary? . . . That's the stuff. Pile them up here, behind Pete. We're going to need a breastworks before we're through with those jaspers out there, or I miss my guess. Pete Riser'll stop just as many bullets as a bag of flour. Could you lift his feet and drag him around straight across this corner?"

Whereupon the recumbent Pete bowed his back and kicked, making odd sounds around the potato which filled his mouth.

For a girl less than five feet tall, Mary Allison displayed considerable strength. She lifted her own weight in flour, did it six times, walling Chip in with his arsenal in the safest corner of the big room.

Just at the last she worked with feverish haste, for the attack which had lulled began again. Within the bunkroom something rammed against the door where the center bar socket was fastened to the log partition with spikes, just above the wooden latch.

As Mary climbed over the barricade and sank down flushed and panting beside Chip, they heard the squeal of the spikes loosening in the log. Another heavy blow and the iron socket stood out from the log. Little Mary looked at Chip, her big eyes full of worried questions.

His brown head moved sidewise in negation. But though his eyes held the hard gleam of the fighter, his lips smiled reassurance.

"They'll bust the door in, give 'em time enough. That front one's a harder proposition. They've dragged a timber in through their fox hole, wherever it is. Take 'em an hour, maybe, but they'll get there, if they keep it up," he said calmly.

"Shall I shoot?"

"No use. You take the rifle and whang away at the front door, if they get busy there again. Aim where you think they'd be standing." And he added, "We can't do much about the window from here—not unless some ambitious cuss tries to crawl in."

"But they'll be coming in from that room—"

"Yes," said Chip laconically, "and say howdy to a bullet when they come."

"Oh. Yes, I guess we can stop them from coming very far," she admitted breathlessly, paling a little at the thought. "But if they all burst in together—"

"Well," said Chip practically, "load me a bunch of six-guns and lay them here in my lap where I can grab them easy. And if you could pull that sack over an inch or two and give me a wider crack—"

"I'm afraid they might shoot through."

Chip gave an impatient grunt. "It's a big room, Mary, and they'll have to locate us in it, first. And I'll *know* where to aim."

"Oh." Then, after a wordless interval, "What if I got fresh candles and set them over on that side of the room? They'd light up the doorway—"

"Swell. Make this corner dark, then. By thunder, we need every little trick we can get."

While the battering upon the door continued, little Mary Allison gathered a handful of candles from the box just behind her, lighted them one by one and set them in a row, four on each side of the door where the center bar had already spilled out of its crazily tilted socket and hung aslant and useless across the besieged door. With her corn-yellow hair falling loosely beside her face, and her black riding skirt streaked and spotted with flour, she looked like a Cinderella lighting tallow candles for Christmas.

"Now, I can't think of anything else to do. Can you?" she asked simply, coming back to their corner.

"You could give me a drink and put the water bucket in back of this wall."

"Oh." Commiseration wailed in her voice. "Do you feel any fever coming on?"

"Nary a fever," Chip lied and drank the dipper dry.

"That cut hurts you, I'll bet."

"Not a darned bit. I'm feeling fine."

"There's an awful lump on your forehead," she said remorsefully. "Big as a banty egg. How does it feel?"

"Fine as silk."

Mary eyed him attentively. "You're pretty fine your-self—if you weren't such an awful liar," she said at last. "Shall I take the rifle and go over and draw a bead dead on the place where that hammering is?"

"You'd probably get yourself a couple of outlaws, all right."

"I bet so, too. Well, shall I?"

"Want to?"

"No-o—not unless you want me to. It would be murder, kind of, don't you think?"

Chip snorted, choking back a laugh almost hysterical, what with his rising temperature and his fear for the girl.

"Is war murder when you fire at the whites of their eyes?" he asked roughly.

"No-o—this really is something like war, isn't it?"

"Hell, this *is* war!" And had Mary known him better, she would have realized the oath betrayed the fever he denied. For Chip Bennett's code did not permit swearing in the presence of nice little girls, even when their faces were smudged with gunpowder smoke.

"Yes, I guess it is. And if I thought we had to fight it out to a finish, I'd get out there and shoot 'em while I had the chance. But—"

"It's fight to the finish, all right." Chip's voice was grim; grim and terribly tired all at once. "If we don't get them, they'll get us. Don't kid yourself they won't."

"Well, but if we hold them off till morning, I'm just sure papa and the boys will come after me. I—I knew it was kind of risky when I started out this morning, so I sort of prepared for it."

"Yes?" Chip's eyes were intent, watching her face.

"Well, yes. I had some old gloves I was going to burn up. The squaws make me lots of gloves and moccasins—so instead of burning them, I just stuffed them in my saddle pocket. Just in case, you know.

"So when that man Poppy and Ed Hartman rode up on me, about five or six miles from home, I—I sneaked the gloves out and dropped one whenever I had a chance."

"Oh." Chip's tone revealed his complete letdown. "And if they scurrup around and happen to find one of your gloves, I suppose in the course of time—"

"Oh, no. Not Papa and the boys. When I didn't come home—well, say by four or five o'clock, they'd start out after me. And they'd take Shindee. He's the best bear dog in the country. You see, I dropped the first glove—I guess I forgot to say—right in the trail where it strikes up into these mountains. They couldn't help seeing it. And of course they'd tell Shindee to go seek Mary—

Her voice broke with startling unexpectedness. And suddenly she was just a frightened little girl again, hiding her face within the crook of her arm, as she leaned against the rough stone wall and cried with low, whispery sobbing that shook her slim little body and made Chip want to get up and kill, burn, slay—take little Mary Allison up in his arms and carry her home where she belonged.

But he could do none of those heroic things. His left side was laced with red-hot irons, and when he moved he started wet little trickles seeping out of the wound. The measured thudding against that stout old door went on, punctuating her sobs now and then with a wrenching squeal, as a spike gave way a little more.

She cried herself out, stealthily wiped her tears on a fold of her riding skirt, and lifted shamed eyes to his.

"I guess you think I'm an awful fool," she said, with a catch in her voice. "I don't know what made me start bawling like that. I don't—"

"That's nothing," Chip said gruffly, because his own voice was not too steady. "I'd bawl myself, I reckon, if I thought it would do any good."

She shook her head at that, smiling ruefully as she tried to smooth her yellow hair that shone in the candlelight, making a spot of brightness in that dark corner.

"You never would. You've got sand and I haven't. But it just seems as if papa and the boys never would get here. Do you suppose they will?"

"I'd tell a man!" said Chip, and squeezed her hand. "And we'll just hang and rattle till they come."

CHAPTER TWENTY-SEVEN
A PRESENT FOR A LADY

What time the door gave way they never knew. There had been intervals of quiet, when the attackers apparently rested and talked things over, perhaps attended to wounded men. Now and then shots were fired outside, but these Chip had decided long ago were not very effective. By the time the bullets bored through the planks they were pretty well spent, and while they ricocheted from the rock walls where they struck, they generally plunked with not much force. During the night, they had escaped many such.

While the door still stood, they had heard again the rattle of powder down the chimney which was only a few feet away. Later, a flaming twist of grass came down into the dishpan and expired harmlessly, and Mary giggled.

Chip did not seem to notice it at all. He lay propped against the blanket roll with his six-shooter in his lap, biting his lip and staring at that door where the spikes squealed and gave way, one by one as it seemed to him, dragging out the suspense intolerably. He could hear them talking in there, muttering, reciting poetry, even—

They weren't getting the lines right, and the thing bothered him, got on his nerves. The damned boneheads had better leave Bobbie Burns alone, if they couldn't get him any straighter than that. What they were trying to say sort of applied to themselves, if the damned chumps only had brains enough to realize it.

When he couldn't stand it any longer, he shouted the two lines they boggled the worst:

"'Oh, Tam, noo, Tam, thou'lt get thy farin' —
In hell they'll roast thee like a herrin'!'"

and once started, he thought he might as well go ahead and give them all of it; which he did, patiently enduring Mary's constant interruptions when she tried to shush him and make him drink water. Well, that was all right. He was thirsty as the devil.

Crazy as he was, though, he had sense enough to know when the first planks gave way and an arm and gun poked through the hole. He was not too crazy to shoot straight, either. The arm jerked comically and fairly threw the gun into the room. And after that they didn't try it again for awhile, in spite of Chip's jeering invitations: "Come and get it, you blinkety-blink this and thats—come and get it while it's hot!"

And he taunted them with things he would have bitten his tongue off before he would have said in front of Mary, though it was clean, honest, man-sized swearing, every bit of it. "You built 'er strong—now, damn your rotten hearts, break 'er down if yuh can! Come out of your holes, you thus and so's, and get what's coming to yuh! You've got a through ticket to hell—and I'm waitin' here to punch your ticket!" And with a loud raucous laugh he would sing out, "Step right up, gentlemen—plenty of room at the top—bullets for everybody! Who'll step forward and get a bullet?"

And little Mary would brush the tears off her cheek and cuddle Chip's rifle against it, trying to take aim when her eyes were so blurred she could not see the sights at all.

All through the night and into the morning, shut in that dark room with its acrid cloud of powder smoke drifting slowly to the fireplace and out up the chimney. By the dwindled candles she might have known that day had come, but she was too distraught to think of counting the hours that way; and Chip, with his left side a torment of searing pain, knew and thought nothing at all save one thing—to shoot every damn son-of-a-gun that poked his head in through that shattered door.

And then a dog barked, off in the grove, and there came a fusillade of shots, and a man outside yelled something to his friends inside. Chip paid no attention to all that. He was busy watching that bunkroom door, the pupils in his bloodshot eyes drawn down to pinpoints, his gray lips pulled tight across his set teeth. To everything else, even to Mary beside him, he was blind and deaf and dumb—but his finger was crooked on the trigger of his gun, which he had laid across a bag of flour, and the barrel did not waver.

Mary heard the sounds like one waking from nightmare. She nearly shot her own father, however, because he walked up and hammered on the door and she had for hours schooled herself to shoot when anyone did that. Babe Allison saved himself by shouting, "Mary! Mary! Are you there! Mary, answer me!"

As she climbed shakily out of the corner, Chip roused to mutter, "Right—this way. Get your ticket—for hell!"

It was with some difficulty that she persuaded him to let go of the gun before he shot one of their rescuers by mistake.

Billy Burns came out of the bunkroom and stood with his hands on his hips, looking down at Chip. And Chip blinked and focused his bleary eyes on Billy, recognized him and tried to grin.

"I—don't know about the horses yet, Mr. Burns, but I've got your third man in there. Had to shoot him. Sorry. He's the fellow I saw light a match, down in the pass that night."

Billy Burns pulled his mouth away down at the corners. "By the look of that room, you sure got yourself a mess of outlaws, boy! Most of 'em's got a bounty on their pelts. Fellers in there I been wantin' to see awful bad. Guess you can keep that star permanent if you want to. Way you've got of glommin' horse thieves ain't slow. I—"

"Nothin' doin', Billy," Weary Davidson cut in decisively. "Chip, he's got a job waitin' for him any time he's able to ride and swing a rope."

"Hunh. Forty-dollar a month job. He can ride with me and make—"

"He's got to stay at our place till that awful gash in his side is well," Mary interrupted him. "He's not going to chase outlaws, anyway. It's too dangerous. I guess papa can find work for him—"

"Mamma!" Weary murmured and looked from one to the other curiously. "There's worse dangers than chasin' outlaws, if anybody should ask yuh."

"I'd like to know what," Mary retorted, but she turned away immediately and did not insist on being told.

"I wouldn't go out there if I was you," Billy Burns mildly admonished. "There's quite a considerable cleanin' up to do around here before it's—er—persentable for a lady. Musta been kinda excitin' around here last night."

"It was, sort of," Mary admitted, too concerned over Chip to faint or have hysterics now, when it was all over. "But they couldn't get in. We made it too hot for them."

"Yeah, I see yuh did," Bill Burns said dryly and went out.

There was, as Billy said, quite a lot to be done around the place. Burt Thompson's gang was shattered beyond the point of reorganization, for they had chosen that particular night to foregather in the stone house, either to celebrate their last depredation or to plan the next one—if Billy Burns got the truth out of a survivor, he kept it to himself. At any rate, they all were there, and they had been altogether too persistent in trying to batter their way inside. Concentrated before the two doors and the one window, two guns

235

could—and did—work a terrible havoc.

Just how terrible, Mary never knew. Nor did Chip, until much later. It was easy to talk instead about all the stolen horses which the Laughing Water men rounded up in that meadow; easy for Weary to talk about the Flying U and all the trouble he had had rounding Chip up—

"—and I guess we wouldn't have found the way in here at all, in spite of the dog, if I hadn't spotted your Mike horse in that gulch. Or if we did get in here, we wouldn't have known you was here too. But quick as I saw the brand and recognized the horse, I knew darned well you'd got yourself in some kinda jackpot. So we come a-runnin'. Had to leave our horses back up the gulch."

"Then how are you figuring to get outa here?" Chip sighed, as if that problem looked as hopeless to him as a trip to the moon.

"Way the rest of 'em got in. We'll handle that, all right." And suddenly it appeared to dawn upon Weary that possibly he would not be missed from that room for a while and that he might make himself useful elsewhere. So he pulled his hat over one eyebrow and strolled outside, slanting a knowing little side glance at Mary as he went.

That intrepid little pioneer was cooking breakfast, chiefly because she wanted Chip to have a bowl of gruel, which she was stirring to a creamy consistency while the boys talked. It must have been ready for some little time, because Weary was no sooner gone than she came with a small tin basin and knelt beside

Chip, blowing across a spoon of the gruel to cool it.

"Mamma always feeds folks gruel when they're sick or hurt," she said soberly. "Taste and see if there's enough salt."

But Chip was not interested in gruel just then nor in how much salt it might require. He had beside him a blue velvet case which he opened with his good hand while his eyes fixed upon her face.

"Lean over. I want to see if this won't go round your neck. If it don't, I'll get some more—"

In haste she set down the basin. "Why, it's all gold nuggets. Where in the world—?"

"Some fellows I know made me a present of it. Try it on."

"Why—why, but if they gave it to *you,* they wouldn't want—"

"I sure never would wear it for a watch chain, that's a cinch. It looks to me like a—a present for a lady. Bend down here. You've got such a slim little neck—"

"But Chip, I—"

"You keep still. It isn't your put-in, little Mary. Fits, don't it? I'll have to get a clasp put on in place of that hook and bar, and then you can wear it—always." He was very busy with his one usable hand, fussing and fixing and measuring that chain of nuggets round her neck. His mouth was not tight now but half smiling, in spite of the fact that his side was raising particular hell with him. His eyes shone.

"But the charm—I couldn't wear that."

By the chain he pulled her head down and down,

until their lips met. "I'll wear the charm myself—if you'll give me a lock of that yellow hair to put in it. I want—" he kissed her again "—I want that little curl right in front of your ear."

So the Duncan boys probably would have been pleased with Chip's use of their present, after all.

And another thing demonstrated at that time was the ease with which trouble is forgotten when love appears. Little Mary Allison had twinges in her right shoulder, to remind her that the recoil of a rifle may become very painful, and Chip had a four-inch gash in his upper left side to remember the night by. But even these were forgotten while they counted the nuggets in the chain and planned just how the clasp must go on, and looked into the locket and discussed gravely whether he could draw a picture of Mary small enough to fit inside and still look anything like her.

Billy Burns started to come in, changed his mind and shooed Weary back, saying not a word.

Center Point Publishing
600 Brooks Road • PO Box 1
Thorndike ME 04986-0001 USA

(207) 568-3717

US & Canada:
1 800 929-9108